FIC
BRICKER

 W9-CND-457

SINS
OF THE
PAST

SINS
OF THE
PAST

•

Sandra D. Bricker

FIL
BRICKER

Rutland Free Library
10 Court Street
Rutland, VT 05701-4058

AVALON BOOKS
NEW YORK

© Copyright 2003 by Sandra D. Bricker
Library of Congress Catalog Card Number: 2003093923
ISBN 0-8034-9624-9
All rights reserved.
All the characters in this book are fictitious,
and any resemblance to actual persons,
living or dead, is purely coincidental.
Published by Thomas Bouregy & Co., Inc.
160 Madison Avenue, New York, NY 10016

PRINTED IN THE UNITED STATES OF AMERICA
ON ACID-FREE PAPER
BY HADDON CRAFTSMEN, BLOOMSBURG, PENNSYLVANIA

In honor of Girl Power.
I miss you, Mom

For Carolbelle
(mother of my God-daughter, Becca!)

*"Entreat me not to leave you, or to turn back
from following after you; for wherever you go,
I will go . . . and your people shall be my people,
and your God, my God."*   *Ruth 1:16*

I always knew, from the very beginning.
I just didn't know how BIG it would be.
You're brave, and you're kind,
and you've stirred my spirit by your faithfulness.
You are the dearest, most loyal friend I could ever
hope to have.

And for Jemelle & Marian

*"Grace to you, and peace . . . I thank God upon
every remembrance of you."*   *Philippians 1:3*

I feel honored to get to see inside the hearts
of two such truly exceptional women.
Your loyalty and encouragement drive me on.

ACKNOWLEDGMENTS

Special thanks to Roanne Eisenbise,
without whom this novel would never have been written.

And to my sassy little editor,
Erin Cartwright,
who takes and returns jabs in such a charming way
that I've begun to relish our sparring process.
You're just the coolest, Erin. Thank you.

Prologue

Lorraine pulled hard at her senses, yanking and tearing for some sort of reason or insight that would make the whole nightmare either come together logically or completely disappear.

She crawled along the dark tunnel in relative blindness, as hundreds of shards of metal and wooden splinters made their way through the sweater material of the once-elegant angora dress. She couldn't be held back by the mere pain of it. If she were to allow that, she would be held back indefinitely by an infinite amount of further pain, of that she was certain.

She could hear his voice far behind her.

"Break the door down if you have to!" he bellowed. "Just get me in there . . . Now!"

She knew that tone, and it made her move even more quickly through the shaft. It spurred her on somehow and she was able to forget the pain. The only thing she could sense in or out of her entire body was the overriding desire to escape him before he snuffed out what little life there was left to her.

"Lor-raine!" he called from somewhere in the enormous

house, and the power of his voice shattered her from the inside. She was the glass and he was the operatic singer, the expert at hitting just the note that would bring about her sundering demise. That's the way it had always been. Always, until this night.

She fought back the urge to curse the tight space for, despite its diminutive size and its overwhelming deprivation of fresh air for her faltering, burning lungs, it was her only escape.

"Lor—raaaaine!!"

She shut her eyes tight and continued on without wavering, without looking back either physically or emotionally. Her fingertips were now bleeding as she pulled herself along through the tiny tunnel, her knees scraped and crimson, her elbows a meaty, blood-soaked mess. She ignored the pounding footsteps above and below her, alongside her and around her at every angle.

His henchmen were zealously in gear throughout the compound, and Lorraine knew she had to keep focused if she planned to escape. And she did plan to escape. It was all she had thought about for the last year of her life.

The scenarios turned over and over in her mind's eye as she proceeded . . . the fantasies, hopes, dreams and prayers for her escape. Freedom seemed so far from her now, yet so close that she could smell its inviting perfume.

The simple pleasures of choosing peanut butter and jelly for dinner over a four-course monstrosity that left her feeling bloated and ill . . . a walk into a library where all the world beckoned to her, and wherein she alone made the choice of what to read . . . not to mention the peaceful escape of a full night's sleep without fear of *him*.

Harrison Carmichael had the odd capability of going from silence to violence, from quiet to instant detonation, in the time it would take a calmer man—*a saner man!*— to wink, or brush away a buzzing insect. Pounding fists, slams to the floor, screams that arose from so deep inside her that she didn't recognize they were actually coming from her, had become so commonplace that she had begun to shut down automatically when they came about.

She would stand back and watch in horror as Lorraine Carmichael, the once-beautiful and joyous young wife of millionaire Harrison Carmichael, was transformed into a savage, grisly heap of blood, tears and screams. And then the search for the silence that she always prayed for . . . but never was found. Never a moment of peace. And her lack of peace had become nearly as overpowering as the thunderous and now-regular outbursts of violence.

No more, she promised herself as she had a thousand times before. But this time she meant it. Something inside her had been torn, like a flag in a hurricane, and she swore before God that it would never happen again. It was a solemn oath, a promise whose fragrance was still fresh upon her spirit when she'd walked in on Harrison and his associates.

It had been innocent enough. She hadn't even known he had guests in for the evening, but it was not his style to wait for an explanation. He had snatched her by the hair in front of them, and she'd felt the heat of her own embarrassment mingle with the excruciating pain as he dragged her down the hall and up two flights of stairs. When she heard the key turn in the lock, the way it had a hundred times before at least, Lorraine swore out loud for the last time.

"No more, Harrison!" she had shrieked, and she'd meant it. Not one more time would he humiliate her, degrade her, abuse her. Not one more time would he leave her there alone to wait for what was sure to come next. And each time he returned to that room was more deadly than the time before it; not just to her body, but to her spirit.

Before Harrison could conclude his business and return

to the bedroom where he'd locked her away, she'd scrambled to the window and flung it open. The night air stung as it rasped the scrape he'd left on her arm. Fear had clouded her for one long moment, but she'd shaken it off like the sun does to haze on a winter morning. She'd gone over the plan dozens of times . . . *She could do it. She had to. And now was the time.*

She groaned as she pushed carefully against the armoire standing beside the door until she had it firmly in place. Right where she wanted it to be, where she had imagined it to be a thousand times as she went over her planned escape in her mind. Then came the bed, right in place against the armoire, followed by the chair and the bureau. One at a time, slowly, as quietly as possible, until an army of furniture footmen held the door securely impassable.

Underneath the bed, right where she'd left it, the roll of linens tucked carefully into the plastic storage bin that had once held sweaters packed away for winter. She quickly tied one end to the bedpost and tossed the other out the window, yanking tightly at each section before it went over. Then, without a single sound to betray her, she produced a pair of tennis shoes from the closet shelf. Plucking the screwdriver from inside them, she quickly stepped into the shoes and tied the laces tight, then cautiously climbed upon the dresser.

The heating and air conditioning ducts were just large enough for Lorraine to crawl into, and it took only a moment to replace the vent before scrambling on her way toward the other end of the house nearest the woods.

"We've made it in through the window, sir," she heard someone say from below her. "It looks as if she's escaped the property. Would you like to come and assess the situation?"

"Of course I would, you idiot. Lead on. Quickly."

When she finally reached it, Lorraine thought her lungs

were going to burst from the influx of clean air. She slammed the vent hard three times with her fist before it fell forward, and she caught it just a moment before it might have tumbled three stories to the ground outside. Hiking her dress up around her thighs, she carefully scaled the edge of the roof to the drain pipe, and slid noiselessly down to the trellis and climbed to the ground.

With fresh resolve and freedom clear in front of her, she ran as fast as she could across the grass. It seemed like a mile before she finally dove through the hedge and into the cover of forest.

The duffle bag was right where she'd left it beneath a pile of brush and leaves, and she didn't bother to stop and look inside. She just snatched it up by the strap and it flew along behind her as she ran through the woods. Anyone watching her would have likened her to a rabbit the way she expertly hopped along, dodging trees, vaulting over downed limbs and maneuvering near-misses with the ease afforded her by many, many practice runs.

This time she wasn't running the stopwatch on her escape. This episode was the real thing, and she was making her best time yet!

Chapter One

"**S**hut up, would ya!" Ray peeled open one eye, just long enough to glare upward at the squawking gull sailing overhead. "Beat it!"

The bird's own brand of rebellion was a cacophony of screeching expletives.

Gull language for telling a man where to go, no doubt.

Ray cranked the lever at the side of his deck chair, propping himself upward with a groan. If that shrieking bird and a raging hangover weren't more than enough to start off his day on the wrong side of the boat, did the blasted sun have to be so jovial and bright as well?

He squinted his throbbing eyes and took a look around. Half a dozen empty beer bottles littered the deck around his chair, not to mention the fully drained bottle of Cuervo Gold toppled over on the table beside him. Aha! That explained the slightly Latino rhythm to the pounding in his head.

There had been a hundred mornings like this one since he'd taken up residence on the rundown houseboat he now called home. The marina glistened at him, and he groaned again. La Jolla, California. It was a beautiful place on better days, but a little too chipper for a morning like this one.

Ray pushed himself up to his feet, then bobbed clumsily for a moment before taking that first step.

A shower would do him some good. Then maybe a walk down the dock toward the diner for some sustenance. After that, maybe some fishing. The notion of heading into the office didn't even dawn much any more, and he wondered how long it had actually been since he'd darkened the doorway marked with blocked white lettering.

RAYMOND MARTIN. PRIVATE INVESTIGATOR.

So private, in fact, that you can't even find him.

Ray chuckled at his own little joke as he lumbered across the deck, instinctively lowering his head to clear the opening to the cabin stairs. It had taken him several weeks to develop the habit, but a few dozen cracks on the noggin were all it took to remind him what it took to pass six feet of man through five feet and 10 inches of doorway.

"Raymond Martin?"

Ray paused on the stairs, then peered out into the cruel sun.

"Excuse me," the shadow of a man called out from the dock. "Are you Ray Martin?"

"Who's asking?"

"Daniel Cort," the man replied, extending a square something in the air toward him. The harsh glare of the sun reflected off the badge and made the announcement before Daniel Cort ever had the chance.

"FBI."

Raine felt as if she could curl up right there in the back office and go to sleep. It was a blustery Ohio day, and the cloud cover remained dark and a bit gloomy.

Gloomy, that is, by anyone else's standards, but not hers. This was Raine's kind of weather! Although it was too early for snow, she looked eagerly forward to her first winter in her new home. Walt Whitman, Ohio. It sang as lyrically to her that day as it had the very first day she'd seen the sign welcoming her.

Raine twisted a lock of shimmering chestnut hair around her finger and looked dreamily out the window through misty emerald eyes. The town was her miracle, and she'd never failed to thank God for it a single day in the nearly three months since she'd arrived.

"Hello?"

She hadn't even heard the jingle of the bells hanging from the front door, and she shook the weather from her vision as she headed through the navy curtain and stepped out into the bookstore.

"May I help you?" she asked, and then the smile faded to something akin to awe as the customer's deep brown eyes met hers.

"I hope so," he said and beamed at her, and Raine felt her heart skip a beat or two inside her chest. "I'm looking for a birthday present for my aunt. She's a very big fan of mystery and suspense. Can you help me?"

"I think so," she said, holding back the urge to run her hands through that wave of dark black hair that fell across perfectly arched eyebrows. "Follow me."

His long, lean frame seemed to loom over her as she scanned the mystery section, and she guessed that he came in right around the six-foot-tall mark. When she looked up at him, the fluorescent lights overhead turned the brown of his eyes to deep ponds made of chocolate starlight and glitter.

"My aunt loves the written word," he told her as he feathered back the wonderfully unruly tuft of hair that immediately returned to its place across his brow. "I'd like to get her an author's set perhaps. Something in hardback."

"How about Agatha Christie?" she suggested, forcing

herself to look away. "We have a set of four on sale right now."

"Agatha Christie," he repeated in a deep, raspy tone that set Raine's pulse to racing.

She reprimanded herself severely several times as she wrapped up the set of books with sienna paper that made a good match with the stranger's compellingly beautiful eyes.

How could she even be thinking the kind of thoughts she was thinking just then? He was innocently scanning the rows of books in the how-to section as the little flutter at the center of her stomach caught her by surprise.

"Do you live here in town?" she asked the stranger casually.

"No," he replied, and turned to meander slowly toward her. "I was born here, then spent summers here as a child visiting my aunt, but I haven't been back in years."

"Came back to visit the aunt for her birthday? Now there's a good nephew."

"If I were such a good nephew, I wouldn't have waited so long to come back." He grinned. "But Aunt Grace is getting on in years, and—"

"Grace?" she asked. "Grace Martin?"

"Yes," he straightened. "Do you know her?"

"Know her? She's my landlady! I rent a room in her home over on North Shore."

"You're the famous Raine Sheridan," he chuckled. "My Aunt Grace's letters have been filled with tales of your adventures. She told me how you took her out on the lake and sketched her portrait. And I believe she's teaching you to quilt."

"I'm not a very good student, I'm afraid. Not terribly patient like your aunt."

"It's more your companionship than your skills, Raine.

You've been a great comfort to my aunt since you've come to Walt Whitman."

"She's been the comfort," Raine said as she lowered her eyes to the counter. "She's saved me in a lot of ways. But I didn't know she had a birthday coming up!"

"Yes, in a couple of weeks," he replied.

"This set of books is a perfect choice for Grace. They'll compliment her collection beautifully."

"Are you alone here?" he asked her, looking around and settling on the navy curtain that led to the back.

"Yes, I'm afraid so." She wasn't quite sure what he was getting at, but a sudden surge of inexplicable hope sizzled through her every nerve ending.

"When do you close?" he continued. "I'd love to go and get some coffee if you're free. My Aunt Grace is the only family I have left, and I'd be very interested in hearing about how she's been getting on."

"It's my turn to cook supper," she explained. "And I have a wonderful stew planned for this windy day. Why don't you join us and see for yourself. Have you seen Grace yet?"

"Yes, I have. But you know her. She'd never tell the truth about her health or about limitations of any kind."

"Right." Raine laughed. "I'll phone Grace and ask her to get it started, and we can grab a cup of coffee down the street after closing. Then you come along to the house and join us for dinner."

"Sounds like a plan." He nodded graciously. "When do you close?"

"The owner will be here to take over at six."

"All right then. I'll come by at six and we'll walk down together."

"Okay."

She tried to hide the blush of heat that crossed her face

in shades of amber and crimson, but it was too late. She knew he'd noticed.

"Wait!" she called as he began to pull the door open. "What's your name?"

"Ray Martin," he tossed back as he tucked the package of books under his arm. "See you at six."

She found Ray Martin more than just remotely attractive. He was captivating; intriguing behind those mesmeric eyes of his. Yet there seemed to be something dangerous lurking just beyond the warmth. It set her on edge in a way, and she wondered if she'd been too hasty in accepting his invitation. After all, even the most innocent relationship was a complication she couldn't really afford to develop.

Warning herself against any thoughts that spanned beyond coffee and that night's dinner, Raine leaned over toward the phone.

"Grace?" she breathed into the receiver once she'd dialed the now-familiar number. "It's Raine."

"Yes, dear. I was just thinking about you."

"I've just met someone you know."

"Well, he can take a hint after all," the old woman cackled. "He was poking around about my birthday, and I tried to subtly turn him your way. You're talking about Ray? You met my nephew."

"Well, he's invited me to join him for a cup of coffee here in town after work," Raine explained.

"Oh, good! I hoped you two would be friends."

"So it's safe then," she teased. "I don't have to worry about being robbed of my millions or my virtue being compromised or anything like that?"

"Well, dear, I can't speak for your virtue, but I would consider Ray a very safe companion, yes."

"Would you mind starting the stew then? Say around five-thirty? Everything's chopped and ready in the fridge. I'll be home to finish it up by around seven."

"Sounds fine, puppet. You and Ray have a wonderful time then."

"Thanks, Grace. See you in a little while . . . Oh, and, Grace?"

"Hmmm?"

"We'll talk later about why you never told me that you had a birthday coming up."

Raine grinned at the familiar click of the tongue that followed.

"The older a woman gets, the more likely she is to want to forget her birthdays, dear. They come around faster every year. I'll be worth something soon. Like an old fossil."

"We are going to celebrate," Raine warned her. "I'll see you soon."

"My aunt tells me you happened across Walt Whitman on your way somewhere else," Ray offered, and then paused to take a sip from a steaming cup of cafe au lait. "Where were you headed?"

"Somewhere huge," she replied, then leaned back in her chair thoughtfully. "Chicago, I guess."

"Just traveling with no plan at all?"

"Something like that."

"Running away, or running to something?"

"A little of both," she managed, then determined to turn the subject as quickly as possible. "What about you? Grace hasn't told me a thing about you. What do you do for a living?"

"Private detective," he replied nonchalantly, and Raine's stomach lurched forward. He didn't seem to notice her reaction, and for that she was grateful, trying hard to appear casual, nodding as he continued. "Nothing glamorous. Insurance fraud, cheating husbands, that sort of thing."

"Not much call for that here in Walt Whitman, I guess." Raine giggled.

"Oh, I don't know. Husbands cheat in every part of the country, don't they?"

Swallowing, she forced a polite smile, and then punctuated it with the shrug of one shoulder.

"So this is what you were running to? A hole in the middle of Ohio, and a little room in a lived-in old house with loose floorboards and a swing on the porch?"

"Yes," she grinned, and a bittersweet taste inched up the back of her throat. "Only I didn't know it."

"What I meant was . . . Why Walt Whitman?"

Raine paused for a long moment, disguising it with a sip from her cup and a heartfelt sigh. She couldn't tell him the truth. Not even the harmless nephew of the one person she might have trusted in all the world. Even Grace knew only what Raine allowed her to know about her past. No one could ever know the whole truth. It was just too dangerous.

"Why not," she spouted, then leaned forward and pulled her purse up from the floor. "You know, I promised Grace I'd be home in time to finish up dinner. I think we'd better head back."

"Do you have a car?"

"No," she replied. "I ride my bike to work every day."

"I have plenty of room in the back of the Cherokee," Ray offered. "Come on and I'll give you a ride."

"No, thanks anyway," she smiled. "I enjoy the ride. I'll meet you there."

She watched him amble away toward the black Jeep truck parked across the street from The Bookmark. There was something about him. Something she wanted to warm up to that struck her as perilous.

On the ride back to the house, she found herself wondering how long he might be planning to stick around. However long or short the visit, staying away from Raymond Martin was going to be a formidable challenge. But Raine was determined to rise to it as if her very life depended on it. Because it did. Secrets had to remain secrets. That was just the way things had to be. There were restrictions on her freedom, guidelines to her life now.

But at least she had a life. And that was one gift she would never take lightly again.

"That's one thing I'll never forget about coming home to Walt Whitman," Ray told his aunt nostalgically. "The smells of your cooking."

"Well, this is Raine's cooking, dear boy. I'm just putting it on for her."

The two of them exchanged warm hugs in the doorway, and Ray followed Grace to the stove. Taking the wooden spoon from her hand, he began to stir the pot while Grace folded down into one of the chairs at the table.

"So, what's her secret?" he asked her without turning back to look for a reaction.

"What do you mean?"

"She's hiding from something," he claimed knowingly, then reeled to look her in the eye. "Do you know what it is?"

"Not directly," Grace replied, placing one stray hair back into the perfectly smooth gray bun at the back of her head. "But she's known a lot of pain, I can tell you that."

"Why is she here?"

"Oh, Ray, why are any of us here in Walt Whitman? She's looking for some peace, looking to make some sense. That's what our little town offers, and it's why we all stay for mostly our whole lives . . . Except for you, of course."

Ray looked down at the impeccable white tiles of the floor and half-smiled. "It hurt you that I left, didn't it?"

"I'd be lying if I said it didn't. But you made such a fine

life for yourself in California, making police detective and all."

Police detective. Two words that still pricked at him with the fierceness of a straight pin found in the carpet by unsuspecting bare feet.

He'd loved the life back then. He *was* the life. And when it had been taken from him, he hadn't known who to be any more. He'd attained his investigator's license, but it hadn't managed to take away the sting in the least. Being a cop was who Ray was, and being robbed of that identity took away everything he'd thought he'd known.

But this trip back into his past just might play a part in rectifying all that. He had something *they* wanted. And for no other reason than that he had been fortuitous enough to turn out to be the nephew of Grace Martin, he might actually be able to make a trade. He might not regain his life, but he could at least round up what was left of the ashes of his reputation. When *they* went looking for someone they could squeeze, Ray's past troubles had stood up and flagged them down.

"I'd also be lying if I said I didn't always know that you'd return one day," Grace continued, interrupting his inner monologue.

"I'm not staying, Gracie. It's only fair to be up-front and tell you that."

"Whatever you say, Raymond."

Ray teetered at the line between irritation and amusement. Old Gracie just never changed.

His heart was breaking with love for this old woman in the eight hours since he'd arrived back in town. The new lines in her face and the increased gray that covered her head were meaningless. To Ray, she would always be that woman who opened her arms to a rebellious teenager clad in a leather jacket and faded old blue jeans. A youth no one understood or could cope with. A young man-child who was angry at the world, suspicious of everyone in it and who could find peace nowhere on earth except inside the eyes of a silly old woman who exuded unconditional love for him like he'd never imagined was possible. Like he'd never seen again since.

"Grace," he whispered as he shook his head.

"Don't go explaining things away to me," she warned him with a wink. "I think that's Raine."

Ray swallowed the emotion that was building in his chest and made his way from the kitchen, squeezing Grace's raised hand before heading down the hall to the front door. Coming back to Walt Whitman had been the hardest thing he'd ever done, but Daniel Cort had provided him with just the incentive he'd needed. Made him an offer he could never have refused.

He watched her through the window as Raine clunked her bicycle up the stairs to the porch and set it to rest against the house. There was something so exquisite about this woman, something he could never have been prepared for upon meeting her. He couldn't tear his gaze away from her.

Not that she was doing anything exceptionally interesting. In fact, it was quite ordinary the way she slipped out of her sweater and headed back across the porch toward the front door, but it had him locked in, frozen him solid with warm appreciation.

He wrenched away from the window to greet her as she came through the front door, trying to force a relaxed smile to his tense face.

"Hello," he said, taking her sweater and hanging it on one of the brass hooks that stood in the foyer. "How was the ride?"

"Exhilarating," she smiled as she passed him, and he watched as she leaned down and kissed Grace on the forehead upon entering the kitchen. "Why don't you visit with your nephew while I whip up the biscuits?" she suggested, and he heard Grace's melodic agreement.

This was going to be a tough visit to Walt Whitman. Tougher even than the last one because, he feared, leaving again would be twice as difficult.

"Now, I think we should discuss the party we're going to throw in honor of your birthday," said Raine as she poured fresh tea into all three cups on the oblong walnut table.

"No, no," Grace protested. "I don't want a fuss."

"I can't think of anyone more deserving of a fuss made over them than you, Gracie," her nephew concurred. "A party is a splendid idea."

"Where should we have it?" Raine asked excitedly. "Not here at the house because she'll be into the plans so deep that she won't be able to enjoy it."

"Quite right." Grace nodded with a chuckle. "Quite right. Ray, have you been over to the house yet?"

Grace and Ray exchanged what appeared to be sudden jolts of a shared revelation.

"What kind of shape is it in?" he asked her.

"I'm not sure. It's been years since I . . ."

"What house?" Raine interrupted.

"Ray's parents' home is on the outskirts of town," Grace explained. "It's a lovely place, and it belongs to Ray now."

"We'll take a drive out tomorrow," Ray promised, and Raine knew he was promising that she would go along with him. "We'll see what shape the place is in, if it's fit for a party."

"That will be lovely," Grace smiled as she lifted the tea-cup and saucer from the coffee table and placed it delicately in her lap atop her napkin. "You'll enjoy that, Raine, with your love of old homes. It's a three-story brick with old white columns out front, and beveled glass doors out the back that look over acres of green lawn."

"The barn down the hill is where Grace met her husband, my father's brother," Ray added, and Raine looked at the woman tenderly.

"Wallace," she half-whispered. She'd heard so much about him that Raine had trouble remembering at times that she hadn't known him herself.

"Wallace," Grace repeated, then took a long sip from her teacup. "I'd love to see that old place again."

"I've told you before that I'd be happy to fix it up for you and let you move out there," Ray suggested. "You love the old place so much."

"And I've told you before, Ray, that house is for you and your wife when you find her. You'll raise your children there the way you would have been raised had your parents not left this earth so early on."

"Your parents died?" Raine asked, then clipped two fingers over her lips in regret for even asking.

"Are you working tomorrow?"

The change in subject was so abrupt that she almost lost his meaning.

"No. It's my day off," she managed, once she'd caught up again.

"Good, then. I'll pick you up around eleven and we'll drive out to the house."

"Fine."

With that, Raine watched Ray raise himself steadily from the chair, plant a kiss on his aunt's cheek and, with a courteous nod her way, he quickly disappeared out the front door.

"Don't be disturbed," Grace said quietly. "You had no idea."

But Raine was disturbed. That night as she laid in bed, wide awake, her mind pumping thoughts through her head like an automatic rifle, she was indeed disturbed by Ray Martin. Greatly disturbed.

Chapter Two

Bringing Raine to the house with him for the first time was a mistake, and Ray knew it the moment he unlocked the door and stepped inside. It was as if he'd opened a door he'd opened thousands of times, only to walk directly into a thundering waterfall of memories, emotions and pain. And the weapons pierced him through and through.

He hadn't been inside this house since the day after his parents' funeral and, besides the spider webs and dust, it really hadn't changed much.

Ray turned to find Raine watching him closely. Those green eyes of hers were like a cat's, peering into his very soul. Ray looked away before she had the chance to read any of the data lying around inside him, then he laughed.

She probably thinks she's the one with all the secrets!

"Why did you laugh?" she asked, and Ray looked back for only a moment.

"This is my past, and it strikes me funny in a way. Don't you sometimes laugh at your life?"

"Not much," she said seriously, and he was sorry he hadn't weighed the question before he'd asked it.

"This house is beautiful," she said finally. "Your mother had exquisite taste."

Funny, he didn't remember her that way. But, looking around, he knew that it was true.

"She was a beautiful woman. Very warm and loving. A tender person."

It was the first time he'd allowed himself to think of her in those terms in so many years. There was something about Raine that reminded him a bit of her. Perhaps it was the way she looked everything over from top to bottom, including him. Or perhaps it was the way she addressed everything head-on. There were no secrets about how she looked at things, how she sized them up. Only about her past. Only about where she'd come from, about the pain in her eyes when she was forced to look back.

"Would you like to go down and see the barn where Grace met my Uncle Wallace?"

"Yes!" she replied excitedly, and Ray couldn't help but smile. The romantic in her was showing, and it was quite appealing.

Too appealing, actually.

"We're on just shy of twenty acres," Ray explained as they headed across the lawn and over the first of several rolling hills. "There's a pond down below, and there . . ." Raine looked in the direction he was pointing out. "There's the barn."

When she saw it there at the bottom of the hill, Raine couldn't help herself. She took off running like a child who saw something wonderful on the horizon. It was just the way she had pictured it the night she'd heard about Grace's first meeting with Wallace. It was made of redwood, and it needed a coat or two of paint. The handles on the enormous doors were made of old brass, and the inside smelled of something that needed a good airing out.

In the corner, Raine spied something shiny poking out of the bottom of a huge scarlet tarp. She hurried to it and yanked back the covering, squealing with joy at what she found beneath.

"They went on a sleigh-ride that night," Ray told her as he stepped inside the barn. "That's the sleigh."

Its seats were upholstered in torn burgundy velvet and, although the thing showed severe signs of wear, Raine's mind simply danced with ideas about restoring it.

"We could hold the party right here in the barn," she gushed. "And we could restore this sleigh and string white lights on it and set it in the corner. All of the guests could put their gifts on it!"

"Hold on," he cried, trying to slow her down. "Just hold on. I haven't agreed to anything here. This place needs an awful lot of work to get it ready for a party in less than two weeks."

"I'm sorry," she deflated. "I don't even know what your financial situation is, or your personal situation . . ."

"No, it's not the money," he explained. "I just—"

"It's none of my business at all, Ray. I'm sorry."

"Don't apologize."

They fell all over each other like that for several moments, each of them trying to explain, and each of them trying not to say anything at all. Finally, they looked one another square in the eye and began to laugh.

"We're ridiculous!" Raine giggled.

"Beyond ridiculous." Ray shook his head as he chuckled.

"Okay, here's the thing," Raine said straightforwardly. "I have a bit of a background in design. I began to study it anyway . . . in another life . . . and I really enjoy it. I could get this barn in shape in a week's time."

"And the house? Could you make it livable?"

"The house," she said carefully. "I'd have to look it over

on those terms. It would depend on how livable you mean. To move into?"

"Hypothetically. More for Grace, if I can convince her."

"Are you interested enough for me to take the time now to take a look?"

"I think so," he said, brushing that wave of hair back from his eyes just long enough to flicker a smile at her before letting it fall back over his brow. "In any case, it would make Grace very happy if I took some interest in this old place, paid it some attention."

"You have a wonderful home here, Ray. Any attention you pay it would be in your own best interest."

"You have that way about you, don't you?"

"What do you mean?"

"That way of always hitting the nail directly on the head." He half-grinned. "No matter whose thumb is in the way."

"Did I offend you?" she asked sincerely. "I didn't mean to. I don't have any idea what really drove you away from here all those years ago, or what kept you from returning, but this is a beautiful place. And it obviously holds family memories that you wouldn't want to erase. I just think if you're fortunate enough to have something like this to come back to, it's really a shame not to appreciate it for what it is."

Ray looked around at the old barn and smiled. "Maybe you're right."

"I know I'm right!" she nodded. "What's the worst thing that could happen? You'll fix it up and maybe decide to sell it."

"Bite your tongue!" he cried with a bitter laugh. "Grace would have me lynched if I put this place on the market."

"Then maybe give it to her. Let her move in."

"Now that's my thought. But she has her heart set on

my living here with a fairy tale princess and a dozen or so kids to follow."

"You'd need two dozen to fill it!" Raine laughed. "How many bedrooms does it have?"

"Seven," he recalled. "Or eight. And four bathrooms."

"You could convert it into a hotel," she suggested. "Maybe make some money off it if you don't want to live here."

She seemed to have struck a cord in him, and Raine shifted from one foot to the other, wondering if she should interrupt his thoughts. He wasn't speaking out loud, but there was an obvious conversation rolling around inside his head just then, and she debated on whether to say anything, or just disappear.

"I'm heading up to look around," she said softly, and he barely noticed her departure.

She didn't know how long she'd been up at the house before Ray finally joined her, but she had explored every inch of the first two stories of the house and found it to be magnificent. Despite some water damage in the pantry and one of the upstairs bathrooms, the only repairs needed were from signs of wear rather than any real necessity.

The furniture beneath graying sheets was nothing less than sublime, and each room was filled with classic pieces that included four-poster brass and canopy beds as well as armoires and commode-style tables. On the third floor was the *piece de resistance* of the entire house. The master suite.

The whole floor consisted solely of one room besides the exquisite marble bath. It was set up in sections, with a king-sized canopy bed drawing the attention of the squared-off sleeping area, and an oval alcove quartered with love seat and two chairs gathered near a walnut-mantled fireplace and surrounded in carved bookshelves.

"This was my parents' room." Ray sighed from the doorway, and Raine twirled around on her heels in surprise.

"How many children were there in your family?" she asked once she'd caught her breath.

"Just me and my brother," he replied. "He died from pneumonia when I was just ten."

"This house is so huge," she exclaimed. "And only two children?"

"It was my mother's family home. She was the youngest of twelve."

"Ah!" Raine nodded. "That explains it then."

"My parents loved this room," he told her as he ran a hand along the dirt-stained mantle. "My father said this is where they made their plans, where they plotted out their life together. He said it would someday be where I—"

Emotion seemed to reach up from his heart and twist at the words before they could make it out of his mouth, and Raine's own heart wrenched at the sound of it.

"They were very much in love," he went on, and Raine folded her arms across her chest and held on tight, consciously warning herself not to cry upon spying the wistful, faraway look misting over his eyes. "Sometimes I'd watch them out my bedroom window as they went for one of their walks. They would hold hands, and you could hear my mother's laughter echo through the trees all across the far hill. My father would sometimes take her hair in his hands and . . ."

Raine waited, but Ray remained silent. She looked up at him to find that he had dropped down into one of the chairs and seemed to be folded in two. She went to him and placed a hand gently on his shoulder and massaged it tenderly.

"I'm so sorry," she whispered. "This is very difficult for you."

"I've said too much," he said hoarsely, then rose from

the chair and walked determinedly toward the doorway. "I shouldn't have come back here."

Raine stood motionless as his shoes thumped down the stairs in concentrated rhythm. A chill went over her entire body, and she grasped her arms and pulled them tightly into her. She felt oddly as if all warmth had been stripped from her, leaving her exposed and helpless. She could only imagine what it would be like to be confronted by her own past.

Rubbing her arms swiftly, she closed her eyes, then swallowed hard before closing the door behind her and silently descending the stairs.

Raine saw him there in the distance, standing stiffly like a starched shirt on a windless day. There was so much pain lingering inside this man. So much that was unresolved. She fought off the urge to go to him and take him consolingly into her arms.

There had been only two men in her life to speak of throughout her 28 years, her own father being one of them. And neither of them had ever shown an ounce of vulnerability or softness that might have elicited the kind of warm response Ray had been able to stir up inside her in just those few minutes alone with him.

"Perhaps we should go," she offered in a voice so close to a whisper that, when he didn't respond, she thought maybe he hadn't heard her. "Would you like to leave?" she added after a long moment.

He turned to face her and she noticed what were possibly tears standing in his eyes. Or perhaps something brought about by the wind?

No, solid emotion had gelled there, and something akin to betrayal poked strangely through at her.

"Are you all right?" She couldn't help herself.

Ray looked away from her for a long moment, searching the ground for his response.

"I can't do this," he finally managed, and then he was off in long strides across the lawn, toward his truck.

Raine watched him for a moment, not sure what to do. After all, he had been her ride to the house. His march seemed determined yet unstable as he moved away from her on lean legs that seemed to be painted with the faded denim material of his jeans.

The impulse came out of nowhere really, and Raine sauntered after it as if it had been true revelation. Without a moment's thought about it, she took off after him and hurried up behind him just as he pulled open the driver's door of the black Cherokee.

"Ray."

He turned to face her and his gaze melted her like wax. There was grief in his eyes and it seemed to spread out between them like a thin layer of oil.

"I'm so sorry," she told him softly, then moved toward him and wrapped her arms around his neck to pull him close. "Whatever it is," she whispered near his ear, "I'm very sorry."

It was a long moment before Ray flinched at all, and then he slid his arms around Raine's waist and pulled her into him. Desire rose out of nothing and crashed inside her in hot, breaking waves.

They looked into each other's eyes for several long instants, a lifetime and yet only a moment, and then it was clear that they were in sync. Ray's mouth dropped upon hers like a flame, fierce and overtaking. He seemed to be partaking of every inch of her by just that kiss, drinking her in until she thought she could stand no more, and then he moved slightly from her and began to plant tiny kisses on her tender lips, nibbling in quick little bites like a playful squirrel with a treasured nut.

"What . . . am I . . . doing," he managed between kisses, and Raine smiled a smile so broad that he kissed her teeth.

Ray pulled her into him, wrapping himself perfectly around her like a snug, well-packed parcel, burying his face in the volume of her hair until the skin of his nose touched the pearly skin of her throat.

"You smell wonderful," he said hoarsely, but she couldn't speak a word. She felt dizzy. Light and airy, like notes rung out of bells somewhere far away. His touch was searing, and his voice had the quality of sandpaper being spread over with warm, thick honey.

"I . . . apologize." And the funny thing to her was that he seemed sincere.

"For kissing me?"

"Yes."

"Why?"

He looked at her curiously, the half-lilt of a smile rising to one side of his beautiful red mouth.

"Because it was inappropriate," he said as he appeared to pull himself together, straightening his frame and bringing his expression into serious captivity.

"I thought it was wonderful." She grinned at him. "I was hoping, actually, that you might do it again."

He breathed out a mixture of a chuckle and stunned surprise. "Are you always so straightforward?"

No, she had to admit that she wasn't. There was something in the air that afternoon, a boldness that had never come naturally to her before. And so she lied. "Yes. I am."

Raine knew that the moment had indeed slipped away from them as Ray placed his hands on her shoulders and looked at her squarely.

"I have no intention of getting involved with you," he told her straightforwardly. "You or anyone else. It has nothing to do with you as a person, understand . . ."

His words began to run together, like late-night television humming in a dark room just before one drifts off to sleep. Once again, she had been relegated to this. She was Child and some man was Father. She the Student, and he the Teacher. The desire to assume the role of Woman to his Man was almost overpowering, and the disappointment at the reality of the situation nearly staggering.

She recalled the previous day of their meeting, how she had been afraid to even sit in the car with him for the short ride to Grace's house from town. And now she understood the wisdom in that reaction.

Kiss her until she responds, then toss her aside, she assessed as she stared at him. *Pull her in until she's almost there, then set her firmly into line. Lay down the law. Well, no thank you.*

His eyes were as liquid as raindrops falling into the ocean. And he was explaining her away like a meteorologist tracing a storm that had passed.

". . . I'm just not in a position to get involved with a woman at this juncture. I think it would be best if we made like this never even happened."

"I suppose you're right," she interrupted coolly. "I feel the same. Now, would you mind dropping me off at home? It's sunny enough that I'd like to get some work done in the garden."

His mouth snapped shut at that, and he cocked his head curiously. Then, with a curious little smile, he nodded. "Yes. All right."

She'd said her good-byes politely enough, but Raine walked away from Ray as if he'd just confessed to some contagious disease. By the time he made it up the steps and across the stone porch to the front door, she was already in the kitchen with Grace and putting on the kettle for some tea.

"Is Ray with you?" he heard his aunt ask, and he stepped up the pace to the doorway.

"I'm here, Grace."

"Tea?" Raine asked so courteously that it stung.

"Yes, please."

She was somewhat amusing, that little thing, the way she danced busily around the kitchen, her cheeks still stained with the blush of their kiss.

And just why had he kissed her like that? Had he gone insane?

"So, how was the house?" Grace finally asked. "Is it in any shape for a party?"

"W—ell . . ." Ray sputtered, then his eyes met Raine's immediately. They'd been somewhat . . . *distracted* . . . and hadn't even discussed it any further.

"It's a beautiful old house," Raine took over. "I think the barn would be a great place for a party. I even spoke with Ray about doing some refurbishing in the main house."

"Oh, Ray! Is that true?"

"Well, I'm going to give it some thought."

She'd caught him completely unaware and, from the glint of a smile that shadowed her ivory face, he could see that she rather liked it that way.

"I mentioned to Ray that he might want to consider converting the place to a bed and breakfast," she continued as she poured hot water into three cups, her back to them. "That way, it can bring in some income and make itself useful until he stumbles across that woman you're so sure he's going to fall for."

"What a marvelous idea!" Grace exclaimed as she turned to Ray. "This way, the house would always be there for you, ready and waiting."

"It's there for me now," he protested.

"But there are some repairs badly needed," Raine said to

Grace as she joined her at the table, leaving Ray standing in the doorway like an impersonal batch of linen left hanging on the line. "There's water damage from the upstairs bath, and the whole place cries out for fresh paint and wallpaper. A general airing out."

"Why, it's capable of being a little mini-resort, Ray. In the winter, guests can skate on the pond." Turning to Raine, she added, "Did you see the pond?"

"No, we never made it down that far. But we did find this wonderful old sleigh in the barn that could easily be restored to—"

"Oh, the sleigh!"

Heat rose up his neck to his face, and Ray could feel anger swelling in him like lava. Just what was she doing here? He thought he had made it clear to her back at the house that he had no plans to stay on in Walt Whitman. Surely she was aware of the hope she was building in Grace, hopes that were certain to be dashed once his mission was concluded and he could go back to his life. The houseboat called out to him so audibly just then that he could have answered the call right out loud.

Raine was heating up the room like an oven with the door open, and he resented her for it.

"Now what about your accommodations? You're not going to continue on at the hotel when we have this perfectly massive house right here, are you?"

"Huh?"

"Raymond, if you're not able to stay on at your own house, you'll come and stay here. Raine, you'll make up the guest room for him, won't you?"

Her reaction told him that he was welcomed by only one resident of the Martin house, which suddenly made him want to move in and stay past the new year. Anything to irritate her as much as she had irritated him.

But Ray shot himself a quick reminder of why he was

in Walt Whitman to begin with. Alienating her would do him no good at all. But a little proximity couldn't hurt the cause, now could it?

"Yes, I think I'll accept your invitation," he said, sitting down at the table with them. "As long as it's not a problem for you, Raine."

"No," she replied almost believably. "It's a big house. There's plenty of room here. We'll hardly even run into each other, I'm sure."

As she took a long sip from her teacup, Ray noticed that Raine's hands were trembling.

"I'll check out of the hotel this afternoon."

Raine had washed her hair under the shower and wrapped it in a towel, then ran a steaming tub of bubbles and dropped her entire body down into them. With a body sponge, she repeatedly wrung the hot, scented water over her shoulders and allowed it to fall in rivers back into the tub as soft, cherubic strains of Mozart tickled the walls around her.

She rubbed her skin with the sponge, then rinsed it with a fresh peak of water. It was only at the very tip of her unconscious mind that she realized it was Ray Martin she was trying to scrub away and not some stubborn stain that wouldn't wash free. At the thought of him, she tossed the sponge down into the crest of iridescent foam and leaned back on the inflated bath pillow suctioned to the tub behind her.

Why did he have to traipse into the house, all of his belongings in tow, like some sort of transient invited to stay on indefinitely? It was usually such a quiet, tranquil place to live. But not since *he* had come along. She could hear every noise he made—if she strained very hard. He was a nuisance, an intruder on the joy and congeniality she and Grace had structured their lives around.

A slight *thud!* down the hall drew rage from inside her like a pack of wild dogs responding to the scent of raw meat. It would be like this from then on, she was sure of it. No peace at all.

With that, she reached over the edge of the tub and turned up the volume on the portable stereo by three notches. Then, after a moment, she realized it was too loud for her to enjoy and sheepishly turned it down another notch and a half.

When Raine finally climbed from the tub, she was a bit withered from nearly an hour in the soak. She pulled the plug on the water and watched as it began to swirl down into the drain, then ran a pumice quickly over her feet and elbows, smoothing them immediately with a couple of pumps from the lotion on the back of the commode. She slipped into the deep crimson terrycloth robe that hung on the back of the door, one of the very few signs of her former life, and headed out into the adjoining bedroom.

As she padded across the plum Berber carpet, she pulled the towel from her hair and let it fall to place in full damp waves across her shoulders. She had just pulled back the floral comforter to reveal inviting lavender sheets that were still fragrant with the wind that had passed through Walt Whitman just a couple of days prior when a gentle rapping at the door took her by surprise.

She froze for a moment to listen more carefully. Indeed, someone was knocking at her bedroom door, and she tightened her robe as she crossed toward it to answer.

Pulling the oak door open, she looked directly up into the black-fringed eyes of Ray Martin.

"Were you sleeping?" he whispered, and he looked uncomfortable, like a boy who'd sneaked into the girls' dormitory.

"No. I'm just out of the bath," she replied matter-of-factly. "Can I help you with something?"

"My aunt has retired for the evening," he returned, just as matter-of-factly. "Would you join me in the kitchen for a cup of tea?"

"I don't think so."

"It's in regard to Aunt Grace's birthday," he interjected. "I'd appreciate just a few minutes of your time."

With that, he turned and walked away down the hall. Raine stood in the doorway and listened as he carefully and quietly descended the stairs. She returned the door to its place and latched it before removing her robe and climbing into the pair of black jeans that hung on the hook just inside the closet.

She grabbed a black cotton shirt at random and carried it to the bed where she snatched up a black bra and snapped it into place before sliding the blouse over her head and running her fingers through her hair to let it fall loose.

I'd appreciate just a few minutes of your time.

His voice had grated over her senses with a stout sweetness that caused her to hasten her pace down the hall in bare feet and take the stairs at more of a skip than a step. She paused just before entering the kitchen to straighten as she had watched him do so adeptly that very afternoon, and she walked in slowly, as disinterested as she could manage to appear.

"Do you take milk?" he asked.

"Yes. And a pack of sweetener."

Raine watched him carefully as she lowered into her regular chair at the table. His cotton shirttails were hanging carelessly over the waistband of his Levis, and his bare feet looked as lean and strong as the rest of him. As he turned toward her and joined her at the table, his eyes appeared sleepy, like someone who had been sitting in the dark for a long time and was caught unaware by an intruder who'd flipped on the light.

"I don't know how good this will be," he tried to grin. "I haven't brewed a cup of tea in ten years."

"I'm sure it will be fine," she replied, and she found herself flicking him the hint of a smile.

"I've been giving some thought to the house," he began, and then paused for a long moment. "If you'd be interested in helping me with it, I think it would be a very good investment to turn it into some sort of inn as you suggested."

Raine was silent for a long time, and he finally raised his eyes questioningly.

"If you're concerned about what occurred between us today," he began, but she silenced him with the casual wave of her hand.

"No," she shook her head. "It's just that I have so little free time as it is."

"I'd be happy to pay you," he offered. "Whatever you think is fair."

Raine struggled hard to disguise the peak of interest swelling inside her. The house had remained with her, and she had done battle against dozens of ideas on its restoration that had tried to capture her throughout the day. Restoring an old house and running it as a bed and breakfast had been a dream of hers from a fairly tender age—not that he'd mentioned her running it—but all the college courses and design books in the world couldn't have won her that kind of freedom once she'd had access to the kind of money it would have taken to live out the dream.

"You said you could prepare the barn for a party in a week's time," he prodded.

"Yes, I'm sure I can."

"Then we'll concentrate on that first. I want to give Grace the party she deserves."

"The whole town would turn out, I'm sure." Raine smiled. "Everyone loves your aunt."

"We'll start there then. I'll leave a check for you on the counter in the morning to get you started. The roof seemed to have a leak. And it will need painting, inside and out. And some sort of a temporary floor for dancing, I suppose."

"Oh, a check," she said aloud. "Could you make it out to Grace then? I haven't started an account yet, and she's been helping me out by cashing checks for me."

Ray took a long look at her. "Certainly."

She wondered what he must have been thinking of her just then, but he broke her train of thought by rising from his chair.

"I'll leave all the details of the party to you. I'm sure you'll be far better at organizing this kind of thing than I would be. Good night then."

"Good night," she managed as he left the room. "I'll get the lights."

Each step of his departure seemed to thump directly across her chest. Their conversation made its way in mazes about her mind, and she sat frozen in that chair for nearly 10 minutes before she finally rose and flicked the light switch.

Chapter Three

Raine sat straight up in bed, drenched in her own perspiration and her heart hammering triple time. Her memories of the night of her escape had been only passing ones of late; she'd become an expert at seeing her past coming over the horizon and washing it away with other thoughts, other activities, before it gained too much momentum. But tonight was different. Where had this dream come from? It was so real, so vivid, Harrison's anger so palpable that she had searched the darkness of the room for his presence the moment she'd awoken.

Raine rose from her bed and padded across the cool floor to the bathroom and flicked on the light. The reflection looking back at her was pale and stark, fear still lurking like a cloak wrapped tight around her shoulders.

She closed her eyes for a moment and took a deep breath. Then, willing Harrison back into the coffin of her past where he belonged, she leaned over the basin and splashed her face several times with cold water.

The barn floor had been relaid, and the men were applying the final coat of terra cotta stain to the inside walls.

They were set to start painting the outside that afternoon. It would be a deep shade of redwood when it was through.

The repairs had been made to the roof, and Raine had asked the men to move the dilapidated sleigh outside for her while she went into town and looked at fabric. She had snipped away a swatch of the burgundy velvet that had covered the seats so that she could find a close match, and she'd had the good fortune to duplicate it exactly for just $8 per yard at one of the hobby shops on the main boulevard.

While she was standing in line to have the fabric cut, she noticed a rack of metallic tassels in every color imaginable and placed four of the shiny gold ones in her basket before stepping up to the register. She had already purchased 12 yards of burgundy cord to detail the arms of each of the seats, and the tassels would create the perfect finishing touch.

Raine had been working hard for days on end in order to turn the barn into the perfect shell for Grace's party. Every evening upon returning home, she found another long list of responses to the guest list. There were five yeses to every no, and it looked as if a good 40 to 50 people were planning to attend.

One of Grace's oldest and dearest friends in town, Mary Collinsworth, had offered to bake the birthday cake, and Raine had graciously accepted her assistance. She had wanted so much to do everything herself, but it seemed to become a bigger undertaking with each passing day.

Another thing that grew with each passing day was her overwhelming desire to please Ray. They hadn't spent more than 15 minutes alone together in a week's time, but Raine found herself thinking of him quite often.

As she draped the burgundy velvet over the seats she had torn bare and restuffed with batting, she thought of Grace and Wallace riding along in that sleigh when it was new, two magnificent steeds pulling them along through the snow, Wallace at the reins and Grace his beaming admirer. It was alarming to her, once she'd noticed it, how easily she and Ray had replaced them in that vision, riding along through the crisp night, streams of unspoken declarations of love gliding between their locked gazes.

Her days were filled with the checking and rechecking of lists, party plans and purchases interwoven with her hours at The Bookmark. Her nights were spent well into the wee hours cutting, pinning and sewing the party dress of her dreams. There was a time when such a dress could have been purchased in an hour's time, but she savored every moment of putting it all together for herself now. Her efforts made it all the more hers.

That same burgundy velvet that she'd used to cover the seats of Grace's beloved sleigh served as the bodice, and the full tea-length skirt billowed with yards and yards of black satin and crimson lace. Raine sewed shiny little crystal beads into jaggedly precise place all along the shoulders and down the sleeves until her eyes would blur, then she would put it all safely away on the closet shelf until the next night when she would be able to see it clearly again.

She'd spotted a pair of black velvet pumps in the window of the dress shop next door to The Bookmark that afternoon, then spent two hours meticulously applying the crystal beads left over from the dress to each shoe in a lovely spray across the top with Grace's glue gun, and she burned her fingertips several times before she was through.

Raine was amazed at how much she was looking forward to this party. She wondered if Ray could possibly look as devilishly handsome as she had fantasized that he would, then decided that, yes, indeed he would.

She lay in bed, staring at the ceiling like a child the night before her first day of school. She felt giddy and excited, nervously intoxicated on her own high spirits. She was eager for the night to get on and pass her by so that she was free to kick into gear for the day, taking care of last-minute details, preparing the decorations and stringing the lines of white twinkling lights. The party would be held that evening, and she could hardly contain herself until dawn.

"Is everything in place?" Ray asked Raine over his cup of morning coffee, the first time he'd seen her in two days.

"Yes," she replied excitedly. "The barn looks absolutely beautiful. I've taken today off to spend on the decorations. Why don't you stop over and have a look this afternoon. You can help me inflate balloons."

"What an appealing invitation," he said sarcastically, the sight of himself blowing hard into a hundred or so stubborn balloons dancing before him.

"Helium balloons," she teased. "There's a tank."

"In that case, I'd be happy to stop by. I'll be free around noon. I could bring some lunch, if you'd like."

"Perfect!" she cried, then scurried from her chair and rounded the corner just in time to plant a noisy kiss on Grace's cheek as she walked through the doorway. "Happy birthday, Grace!"

"Thank you, dear," the woman called to her as Raine skipped up the stairs, humming. "I haven't seen her this happy in all the time she's been here in Walt Whitman," she told Ray, then folded into her usual chair in the corner.

"She's definitely in her element out at the house," he commented.

"I believe she must have a background in decorating of some sort," Grace surmised. "The way she pays such vigilance to detail."

"Yes, she took a lot of courses in interior design before she was married," Ray said casually, then shook himself back to attention.

"Did she tell you that?" Grace asked candidly. "She's

never uttered a single word to me about her past, Raymond. Not a word."

"Oh, we were talking about college and things," he tried to say carelessly. "It just came up."

"She was married, then," she continued thoughtfully. "Did they divorce, or was she widowed?"

"Uh, I don't really know."

"It must have been tragic, at any rate," the woman said as she shook her head. "She came to Walt Whitman a scared little mouse."

Several minutes passed before Ray finally rose from his chair. Tucking his hands into both pockets at the sides of his slacks, he forced a smile to the surface. "I'd better get moving then. I'll see you this evening. We'll drive over around six, if that's good for you."

"What a lovely birthday this is going to be." She grinned with a hint of emotional mist rising in her eyes. "Having you home again is the best gift I could have been given, Ray. I've missed you so."

"I've missed you, too, Gracie." He smiled in return and kissed her tenderly on the cheek. "I'm just sorry I stayed away for so long."

"You're home now."

Ray gently massaged her cheek with his thumb before leaving. He passed an exuberant Raine on the stairs, and she bounced past him like a rubber ball.

"This is going to be the best party you've ever attended," she promised as she bounded past. "See you at noon!"

Ray couldn't help but smile. Her joy was somehow contagious. He'd never imagined this playful energy when he'd first been told about Raine Sheridan. Alias Lorraine Carmichael, a name that just didn't fit this girl no matter how hard he tried to put them together.

"See you this afternoon, Grace!" she called, and then the door slammed shut behind her.

"Good day, child," Grace returned, but it was too late. Raine was already well on her way.

Raine found herself checking the time every 10 or 15 minutes until it was finally noon. When she noticed Ray heading over the side of the hill, several paper sacks in his hands, she couldn't resist running to meet him.

"I found an old quilt in the house, and I thought we could sit on it down by the pond and eat our lunch," she offered, the quilt already in hand. "Then, afterward, I'll take you up and spring the barn on you."

Her enthusiasm seemed to rub him just right, and Ray agreed with a shrug and followed her down the hill where the pond was hidden on the other side of the trees.

"The paint job looks good," he told her as they continued. "What have you done to the inside?"

"After lunch, Ray."

"Did you know that the roof needed some repair? I think I forgot to point that out."

"The roof has been repaired," she appeased him. "Now come on!"

The old path led straight through, and Raine wondered if Ray noticed how casually she navigated through his old stomping grounds. The truth was that she couldn't concentrate on much of anything besides his pending arrival that morning, and she'd taken a walk down the hill only to stumble upon the pond she had forgotten Grace had mentioned the week prior.

"How about over here?" she asked, pointing to the spot she'd scoped out only hours before.

"Fine."

Raine spread out the quilt on the grass, and then helped Ray unpack sacks of deli sandwiches, potato salad, packets of pickles and sodas.

"I hope you like corned beef," he offered. "It's my favorite."

"I haven't had corned beef in a month of Sundays!" she exclaimed happily, and then dug into the feast leaving Ray to catch up to her.

"It's perfect!" she added through a full mouth.

"So, how is the party coming?" he asked between bites. "Are we all set?"

"I can't wait for you to see the barn," she cried, and then took a hefty bite out of a huge garlic pickle. "The sleigh is the best part. I painted it and reupholstered the seats. It looks brand new. I've given some thought to the house too, Ray. I've had the time to take a close look around. Once the party is behind us, maybe you can look over some of my notes."

Ray smiled and shook his head. "You're a little dynamo, aren't you?"

"It's just so wonderful to have something creative to do," she replied, staring out over the water. "It's been years since I've had the kind of freedom—" She tripped over her words as she came to a grinding, obvious halt. "Thank you, that's all," she added softly. "Thank you so much."

"For what?"

"For allowing me to do this. For not looking over my shoulder and yanking on the reins."

"It's not my style."

She had thought it was the style of all men. "Well, I'm grateful just the same."

"How about we take a look?" he suggested when the last of the lunch had been devoured. "And then we can get to those balloons you've enlisted me to inflate."

Raine was on her feet in less than three seconds, collecting trash and pulling on the quilt that he was still sitting on.

"Okay, okay." He laughed. "I'm going to have to learn

to be poised and ready around you before I ever suggest moving."

"I can't wait to see what you think. Come on!"

Ray followed Raine up the hill by just a few paces. He admired her tan, muscular legs as they carried her upward, draped sensually by the casual billow of her pink cotton skirt. There was something childlike about her, even at nearly 30 years of age, and he acknowledged the realization that he might have truly enjoyed the nuances of a relationship with such a woman under any other circumstances.

"Come on!" she called back to him as she reached the top of the hill, then scurried to the trash can and deposited what was left of their picnic. "Close your eyes," she invited, taking him by the hand. "Don't look until I tell you."

Normally, Ray didn't indulge in such games, but something about this woman made it irresistible to him. He blindly stumbled after her, recognized the creak of the old barn door, and then took a few steps forward upon her leading.

"Wait . . . Okay, you can look!"

He opened his eyes to find himself ensconced in a world that looked scarcely familiar. The roof had indeed been repaired, and the walls were painted in a rich terra cotta. The floor was partially paneled with planks of rich oak, and strands of hay had been scattered over it to give it a warm, country feeling. In the corner sat the sleigh, looking brand new just as she'd promised, and it was outlined in tiny white lights that were hung throughout the rafters to take on the appearance of billions of twinkling stars overhead.

"I want to scatter bouquets of white balloons throughout the whole structure," Raine said, painting the picture with her hands as she went along, "and then let a couple of dozen loose to the roof with just white ribbons hanging down from them."

"Raine."

She froze momentarily, and when her activity stopped it was to Ray as if the whole world had stopped.

"You don't like it?" She seemed to cave in before him.

"No, no," he assured her. "I love it. It's beautiful. It's far more than I thought you would be able to do in such a short time. You're a genius."

"You mean it?"

"If you can do half this well with my house, you're going to make me a very rich man!"

Raine seemed to reel with relief, and she ran to him and threw her arms around his neck in an embrace. With a gentle kiss to his cheek, she pulled away. Not that he would have minded holding her there a few moments more.

"Thank you." She blushed. "I've had the time of my life doing it."

"What about food and drink?" he asked. "Do we have that all set up?"

"I've ordered a feast from Donovan's in town."

"Wonderful! I've known Sly since I was a kid. He's the best there is."

"He thinks the world of your aunt." She grinned. "I think he's going above and beyond because it's for her. Grace's friend, Mary, is baking the cake, and I've ordered enough beer, wine and cider for a hundred people. When I pick it up later, I'll also get the ice."

"I can help there. You'll have things to do to get ready. Woman things. I'll make the run into town if you'd like."

"Woman things?" she teased, and he laughed right out loud. "I'd really appreciate that. I told Les I'd be in around four."

"Four it is."

"So you'll have just enough time to help me with the balloons."

Ray carried the two helium tanks in from where they

were resting against the outside of the barn while Raine produced a thermos of lemonade from the basket on her bike.

The two of them set about inflating the balloons, and soon had a very good system in motion. Ray would insert the helium and tie the knot, and then Raine would apply the ribbon and wrap it around the brass hook on the wall by the door. In less than an hour, they had nearly a hundred white balloons with long, curly white ribbons ready to be placed about the deep russet room.

"Can I give you a lift home?" Ray asked when they were through. "It's nearly three-thirty now."

"Would you mind?" she asked. "We can load up my bike if I can have a ride over with you and Grace this evening."

He nodded in approval of the suggestion and headed out of the barn.

"It's going to be so beautiful," she said aloud in the doorway before latching shut the door, and Ray agreed.

"You've done a wonderful job, Raine. Thank you."

It was funny to Raine how much those words meant to her, how she carried them with her in the car on the ride home, in the bath and at the mirror as she applied her makeup. Ray's simple thank you had undone her emotions as if he'd sliced the cord that bound them.

So few thank yous had ever made their way to Raine's ears. Rather, demands and commands were what her life had consisted of, perpetual in their presence, constant and consistent. Oh, they'd come in different forms, of course; some of them perhaps even in the guise of suggestions, but they were demands just the same.

You don't really want to do that, Lorraine. Are you tell-ing me what you're going to do, Lorraine?

And so Ray's simple words that afternoon rested upon

her like a lovely sleeping kitten one holds carefully, strokes and enjoys.

You've done a wonderful job, Raine. Thank you.

Even the way he said her name left her warm and joyful, and it ran through her like the haze of some fragrant perfume. She tried hard to remember, then felt certain that no other man had ever thanked her for her efforts the way Ray had.

She imagined that this was the kind of thing she'd been missing all those years locked away. That there were moments of happiness to be enjoyed throughout one's life that would hang like pearls on a synthetic thread to be added to, built upon. This was what true joy was made of, she was certain. Moments. Moments like those she had known since coming to Walt Whitman. To Grace's home. Since meeting Ray.

She had planned on pinning her hair up atop her head, but once she'd removed the electric rollers and the curls fell so perfectly about her face, she decided to let them be free. It matched her spirits.

Raine hadn't worn a speck of makeup besides foundation and blush since her arrival in town, but she was feeling jubilant, much in the mood for a party that night. Dark gray powder enhanced her emerald eyes, and black liner highlighted them all the more. A deep crimson lipstick that matched her dress topped it off, and the one piece of jewelry she had managed to bring along to her new life—a gold choker that had belonged to her mother—sat beautifully still just above her collarbone.

As she slid into the dress she had designed just for Grace's evening, she had a quick flash of how Cinderella must have felt when she got a load of her own new clothes. Raine stared hard at herself in the mirror and could hardly believe it was her. She faintly recognized the woman she saw looking back at her, one she'd thought had died long ago.

"Nice to meet you again," she whispered to the reflection. "It's been a very long time."

Ray's attention was quickly drawn, like a hook pressed cleanly through his jaw. Raine's delicate feet made their way down the steps beneath shimmering dark legs that he longed to caress. The further into view she came, the more out of control his heart raced.

"My . . ." He sighed audibly, and his eyes met hers for one stiff moment before he jerked them away. "Grace? Are you ready to go?"

When he looked back, he couldn't help but swallow hard. It was as if she had somehow caught up his breath at just her mere presence, and the scent of her had transported him several inches above the floor.

"You look exquisite," he said finally.

"Thank you."

"Raine, dear," Grace gasped from the hallway. "You're a vision. Like a fairy princess, darling."

"Thank you, Grace!"

"Doesn't she look lovely, Ray?"

"Indeed she does," he agreed.

Raine sat in the back seat of the Cherokee, and Ray stole glimpses of those magnetic eyes of hers in the rear view as often as he could without her noticing. He felt like a giant batch of soup on the stove, hot and rumbling, and she was the spoon, stirring him to the core.

He'd never seen a woman so beautiful, never known a woman who moved him so deeply.

"You'd better slow down, dear."

He nodded toward Grace and let his foot lighten atop the gas pedal. His thoughts of Raine had brought him upwards of 70 miles per hour. And that was just in the Cherokee. Never mind his racing heart.

It was difficult to picture Raine in any surroundings but these. She was like a young sparrow whose feathers had never been touched by the cold hand of the pain he occasionally glimpsed in her eyes. What horrors had she endured in the life that came before, he wondered.

"Ray?"

"Sorry." He hadn't noticed the red light until he'd already barreled through the intersection.

"Where are your thoughts, dear?"

He didn't bother to answer. His thoughts were right there in that Cherokee. Behind him, in the back seat.

The quartet suggested by Les at the liquor supply store was just what Raine had hoped it would be. Its expertise ran the gamut from chamber music to something with a dance-worthy beat.

As she watched Grace make her way around the room, from one face to another to yet another, an unexpected wave of emotion splashed her suddenly. Grace had been in that town for most of her 70 years, and Raine admired that. Envied it. Was even jealous of it in a way. She wished that she had people who knew her, and that she had known, the way Grace did.

There were people in that room who had befriended Wallace, who had even attended their wedding. Several of them knew Ray's parents, and they remembered when he'd gone to live with Grace, and later when he left town to join the police department in San Diego. Raine couldn't help but imagine him in his creased trousers and starched uniform shirt, a gold badge on the breast pocket, perhaps an officer's cap pulled down low across his dark brow.

There was history there in that old barn, from Ray's past all the way down to the old sleigh that once carried Grace and Wallace across an expanse of snow-covered landscape. The bitter reminder that her own history had long since been washed away, covered over by poor choices and broken dreams, rose up in the back of her throat.

"How about a dance?"

Raine hid the emotion that had overwhelmed her and walked wordlessly into Ray's open arms. He twirled her around the dance floor until she was dizzy, and then he absorbed her into his own body with inviting, muscular arms.

"What were you thinking about just then?" he asked her softly over the music.

"Another world I once lived in," she managed. "Why?"

"I don't think I've ever seen someone look so sad." Then, after a long moment, he asked her, "Would you like to go for a walk?"

She nodded against his chest and he unwrapped her slightly, one arm remaining around her shoulder which guided her out the door to the crisp dark of night.

Lines of cars littered the hillside in perfect symmetry to the front of the barn, and the sweet, silent night balanced it all to the other side.

"Tell me about that other world," Ray suggested, bringing instant tears to attention in Raine's eyes.

"It's ancient history," she sniffed out into the darkness. "A thousand years ago."

"Is there someone special left back there?" he asked carefully. "A boyfriend, a husband. Maybe some children?"

"I left no one behind me, Ray," she said, looking him straight in the eye as tears dropped down her cheeks. "Nothing and no one."

"There's always someone left behind."

"My life began when I got off the bus in Walt Whitman, Ohio," she told him seriously.

"But what made you get off that bus? Why Walt Whitman?"

Raine chuckled at the memory as she wiped the tears from her face with the soft, warm handkerchief he slipped into her hand.

"You really want to know?"

"Yes."

She heaved an enormous sigh, and then fell silent for a moment. "I was on that bus looking for a miracle," she told the moon loudly enough for Ray to hear. "I was staring out the window, praying silently that I could find something to build from. And that's when I saw it. The wooden sign at the edge of town that reads, 'Welcome to Walt Whitman, Ohio.' "

"I must be missing the connection."

"Walt Whitman wrote, 'As to me, I know nothing else but miracles—To me every hour of night and day is a miracle, every cubic inch of space a miracle.' And when I saw the sign, I was reminded of that. It was as if God were answering my prayer right there on the spot. The simple things of life, the mere freedom of living your life and of being alive, that's the miracle. What better place to live than in the town named for the man who wrote those magnificent words?"

"So you just got off the bus and set down your roots?"

"I had intended to find a big city to disappear into. But in that moment when we pulled into town and I was reminded of that quotation, I knew I had the wrong idea. I wasn't supposed to disappear. I was supposed to plant myself like a seed, and then grow from it."

"You're an amazing woman, Raine Sheridan."

"No, I'm not," she said, looking deep into him. "I'm not amazing at all. But I want to be someday."

"You're amazing now," he said as he took her into his

arms. "Right now, this moment, you are the most amazing woman I've ever met."

Ray placed his hand tenderly under Raine's chin and then raised it gingerly to face him.

"Are you going to kiss me now?" she asked him.

"Yes, I believe I am."

"And you won't run away from me when you're through?"

"No, I won't."

"All right." She smiled. "You can kiss me then."

And he did kiss her. Deep and full. He kissed her right down to her toes and back again. Something rang in her ears, but she didn't think to, or even care to, come up for air and find out what it was. Then her knees went weak and she began to buckle, but his waiting arms brought her right back up again. She felt as helpless as a magnet pressed into solid steel.

Someone called to Ray from the distance, and they both ignored it, Ray drawing her quickly into the shadows to continue their kiss.

"Ray? Is that you? Ray?"

"Yes!" he finally called back, breathlessly, and Raine forced herself to back away from him and fell limply against the car behind her.

"Is it time for the cake? We'd like to sing 'Happy Birthday' to her."

"I'll be there in a minute." He waved and then fell back against the car alongside Raine.

After a moment or so, Ray turned and scooped Raine up into his arms, and they both paused to look upward as hundreds of perfect, glistening snowflakes wafted through the air toward them.

"Grace's cake," she managed before Ray placed his lips gently against hers, still warm with desire for her.

"Grace's cake," he repeated. and he gently released her.

As they headed back toward the barn, Ray took Raine's small hand into his and squeezed it. Reeling with the taste of him and the recollection of his touch, she walked in at his side, snowflakes shimmering upon her like a good dusting from a jar of glitter.

Raine could never remember such happiness. As she joined in to sing 'Happy Birthday' to Grace, her hand still folded neatly into Ray's, tears stood in her eyes of jade, causing them to flash as if they'd been dotted with pure starlight.

Chapter Four

On the ride home, beneath Grace's excited chatter to do with everything from the decorations to the refurbishing of the barn to the beautiful dress Edna Parcels had worn, Raine reached up from the back seat through the darkness and massaged Ray's arm. She noticed his reaction to her and took it as a sort of permission to continue, and she thought she heard him audibly groan as he leaned slightly into her touch.

She felt oddly as if she were betraying Grace somehow by carrying on with her nephew like this, under the cover of darkness, unbeknownst to her, but she couldn't manage to keep her hands away from him. She actually found herself swooning somewhat dreamily as she leaned forward and moved her hand on his arm.

"Come to my room?" she whispered as she allowed him to lean into the car and help her out of it, and she was amazed at her own audacity.

"Yes," was all he said, but it was more than enough. His reply shot through her body and blazed into her soul in a quick, hot swell.

Once inside the house, Grace moved beyond them into the kitchen and flicked on the light.

"Anyone for tea?" she asked.

"No." Raine wondered if she'd sounded a bit too urgent.

"Good night, Grace," Ray said, planting a kiss on the top of the woman's head. "Happy birthday!"

"Thank you, dears. Both of you. It was a glorious evening."

Raine hurried into her room and closed the door behind her. She wished she could change into something alluring, but knew all of her nightgowns were damnably functional, either cotton or flannel, and realized a negligee would be inappropriate anyway.

She giggled at the thought of welcoming him in her flannel gown with the tiny white daisies scattered across the hem. Ray would probably not have the callousness inside of him that it would take to laugh right out loud, but she wasn't taking any chances, and so she stayed in the dress that made her feel like Cinderella.

Ray didn't bother to knock. He just opened the door and slipped inside, replacing it carefully and turning the lock. His reaction to her was more than she had hoped for.

"Raine. There's something I've got to tell you." He seemed to struggle with his own breath. "I can't spend any more time with you until you know."

And I can't talk until you've kissed me again. But she didn't dare say it out loud.

She paused for a moment. Something about the way he was looking at her seemed . . . *desperate.*

"What is it?"

Just as his lips parted to release whatever horrible truth he had to tell, he was interrupted by a gentle rap at the door.

"Raine, dear? Are you asleep?"

Ray instinctively backed away from her, disappearing around the bathroom doorway.

"No," she replied.

"Would you mind coming to my aid, dear? I need to pull the pins from my hair and brush it loose. These tired old arms of mine simply aren't cooperating."

"Just give me two minutes," she answered sweetly, shrugging at Ray's reflection beyond the door in the bathroom mirror.

"Thank you, dear."

Ray moved toward her and the two of them fell into an embrace.

"Will you come back to me tonight?" she asked him, fearful that she already knew the answer.

"I think we'd better talk tomorrow."

With that, he planted a warm, moist kiss on her mouth before disappearing into the hall.

Grace's waist-length hair was as silky as if she were a teenager, and Raine normally loved to run the brush through it. Countless other nights she had performed the same simple task before retiring for the night, and she and Grace would chat about this subject or that. But this night she found herself quiet and edgy, in a hurry to get on with it and get back to her room.

He'd said they would talk tomorrow, but she couldn't help but hope that he would slip through the dark house and carefully turn the knob of her bedroom door, as eager as she was to speak of the feelings that were engulfing them.

But what then? Could she really begin a relationship with Ray without telling him the truth about the littered path behind her? And telling the truth to him, or to anyone, was something that was simply out of the question. She'd known that all along.

"There we are," she half-whispered to Grace. "All done."

"Thank you so much, dear." Grace smiled. "It was a glorious party, wasn't it, Raine?"

"It was," she replied softly. "I'm so glad you enjoyed it."

"You were nowhere to be found when I began opening my gifts. I had wanted to thank you for the beautiful hair clip. I'm going to wear it out, you know."

"Good! I hope you do."

"I saw you dancing with my Ray," she prodded, trying to be nonchalant, but failing miserably. "You two make quite the handsome couple."

Raine wanted to protest, she felt almost obliged to protest, but she couldn't manage the words.

"He's a fine man," she finally replied.

"Yes, he is."

"Well, good night."

"Sweet dreams, Raine, dear."

As she slipped out of Grace's room and closed the door behind her, she cast a look down the hall to the next door. *Ray's room.*

She imagined the sweet, spicy scent of him there, the dark gray suit he wore to the party probably hanging on the rack in the corner, her own floral bouquet still lingering upon it, a product of the heat and friction between them earlier in the evening.

These imaginings were so unlike her!

"We'd better talk tomorrow," he had said, and she played it over in her mind as she made her way down the hall to her own room and stepped inside.

She lay in bed in the dark, remembering the way his lips had parted before they were interrupted. Those sweet, beautiful lips that became red as summer apples after he'd kissed her.

Raine wondered what deep, dark secret those lovely lips

had been about to betray. What was it that was so important that he couldn't hold her again until he confessed it? Perhaps there was a wife and several children in the wings somewhere. The thought of it brought about an ache that nearly overwhelmed her. But surely Grace would have mentioned it. Of course, he had been gone a long time. It was possible that even she was not aware of the secret life hanging in Ray's background.

She threw her restless body over like a beach sunbather, gathering up the pillow beneath her head. Fears, scenarios and speculations were tied up in knots inside her, and they began twisting like snakes throughout her mind, whirling frantically like a crazed potter's wheel out of control. When sleep finally found her, it came in the form of a familiar tunnel, long and dark and devoid of air.

Raine's eyes popped open so wide that they ached, and the drum of her heartbeat was thunderous in her ears. Why could she not forget that night? Why could she not leave it behind?

She flipped over, fluffing the pillow beneath her head, then again in an effort to relieve herself of the ache in her temples, feeling somewhat like a flapjack on a sizzling hot griddle. When she could take no more of her own deliberation, she slid out into the cold room and padded toward the bathroom. Even in the dark, she could go straight to it, and she slipped into the heavy terry robe and headed out into the hall.

She wasn't exactly sure where she was going at first. To find a good book to read, to brew an extra-strong cup of herbal tea. She just knew she couldn't lie there a moment longer. It wasn't until she had taken the first three steps that she noticed the flood of yellow light seeping out from the kitchen.

"Yes, I'm aware of that," she heard Ray whisper, and she turned instantly to stone. The tone of his voice revealed agitation, nervousness, and she waited for what seemed like forever for him to speak again.

"I've hardly left her presence at all, I tell you . . . No, I don't think she has any idea at all, but . . ."

Raine's heart began to pound, and she felt as if she were going to topple over. A river of hushed voices and late-night telephone calls flashed back at her like lightning. She wondered how Harrison and her former life could have been so far from her only a few hours before and now were tumbling down upon her so suddenly and consistently, like sharp pellets out of Heaven.

"She goes by Raine Sheridan now," he said clearly, and she covered her mouth to catch the gasp that tried to escape. "I wish you would call her by that name. We don't want me forgetting and calling her Lorraine Carmichael right to her face."

Just the mention of that woman's name made her spin. That woman she was sure she'd set to rest was now right there in that house with her, alongside her, brushing up against her with fists of fire, urgently screaming out to her.

Run! Run!!

Raine backed up the stairs, her hand still clamped tight across her mouth, and when she reached the top she hurried down the hall to her room and slid carefully inside.

"God." It was all she could think of to say. "Please. Help me."

She paced back and forth for several moments in front of the bed, to the bathroom and back again. How could this have happened? How could she have been tangled up in the arms of a man obviously sent by her husband? She began to wonder if Ray was really Grace's nephew. She tried to recall if she'd ever heard a word about him before he turned up in Walt Whitman, but she couldn't think clearly enough to reach back into time.

Would Grace ever have agreed to such a scheme?

She recalled that some of the people at Grace's party remembered Ray from a young age, remembered his parents, his time as a police officer.

Harrison had scads of policemen on his payroll!

How could this have happened? Raine's mind was littered like the site of a carnival, and the fragmented thoughts blew in every direction, this way and that, until there was no order to them. Only chaos and confusion. Disappointment and fear. And then humiliation.

Raine knew only one thing for sure. She had to get out of Walt Whitman as quickly as possible. She couldn't wait until morning. If Ray had been sent by Harrison to find her, he had already done his job. The only next step would be to bring her back to the compound, and she wondered why he hadn't done that already. Surely there had been plenty of opportunities.

Whatever his reasons for waiting, though, Raine thanked God for them. She was not going back to Harrison and that prison he called home. Not ever!

She hurried to the closet and produced from the very back the tattered duffle bag she had brought with her. She had acquired so many belongings since arriving. She knew she would never be able to take them all with her. She would have to leave things, start again in another town. Leaving things behind was becoming a way of life for Raine now.

The pain of it pierced her to the core, anguish pouring out like blood from the gaping wound. All the signs of life, the little things she had taken such pleasure in . . . her bicycle, her books, her party dress . . . all of it would have to be left behind. She filled the duffle with just the necessities once again. Just like before. A pair of jeans. A cotton skirt. Two sweaters. The terry robe she couldn't bear to part with. Her mother's gold choker.

Raine pulled a sock from the bureau drawer and dumped

the contents on the bed. Six hundred and eighty-four dollars. Considerably less than she'd left Harrison with, but it would have to be enough. She would just be more careful now. As long as she escaped with her life, she was ahead of the game once again.

Raine Sheridan would simply disappear into the night and resurface somewhere else, *someone else*. Yet again.

Ray had already put away his second serving of bacon and eggs when he finally decided to go and check on Raine. It was after 11, and it wasn't like her to sleep in much beyond the first light of dawn.

"The party was a great burden on her, dear," Grace said, trying to explain it away. "She's probably exhausted."

He brewed a quick cup of tea and fixed it just the way she liked it. Milk and a packet of sweetener.

"I think I'll check on her just the same."

Ray looked forward to being alone with Raine, even if it was just for a few minutes. He knew just the way she would look lying there in bed, sleep still hovering over her, those wonderful green eyes just opening up for the day. And while she sipped at her tea, he would tell her the truth. He would tell her that she was the reason he'd been sent back to Walt Whitman . . . and that she was the reason he would leave again . . . and that he hoped she would want to go too.

Three light knocks on the door, a quick check to make sure Grace was still downstairs, and he turned the knob and pushed open the door.

The bed was a mess, and so was the room. She must have had as fitful a night's sleep as he'd had.

The bathroom was the same. Bottles, jars and tubes scattered everywhere. He had seen that bathroom the night before and it was tidy as a little shop. Something was wrong.

Ray reeled toward the sink. No toothbrush or toothpaste.

He set the cup of tea down on the back of the commode and hurried out into the bedroom. The dress she'd labored over for so many crosseyed evenings was curled up in a ball at the back of the closet. Empty hangers dangled from the rod between occupied ones. The bookcase in the corner was disheveled, and four or five hardbacks seemed to be missing. Just as she seemed to be. Raine was gone, and Ray felt her absence so keenly that it ached right at the pit of his stomach.

He took the stairs three at a time and landed with a thud! at the bottom. Grace's face curled up with worry the moment he entered the kitchen, and he hurried to the phone and began to dial.

"Raymond? What is it?"

"Raine is gone," he shot toward her, then pulled his attention back to the receiver. "Yes, give me Cort. Right away!"

"Maybe she's gone for a walk, dear. Or into town."

"She's taken some of her things, Grace. She's gone."

"Oh, my . . ."

"Yes, Cort. Ray Martin. She's gone . . . Gone, gone. I don't know. Just gone! Get someone on this right away. I'll go into town and ask some questions. The moment you have a direction, get back to me."

"Ray, what's going on here? Who was that?"

"I'll have to explain to you later," he promised, then squeezed her hand. "I'm sorry. I have to go."

The worry on his aunt's face buzzed about his conscious thoughts the whole way into town. He left a trail of dust in the path behind him as he traveled the back road at nearly 60 miles per hour.

"Raine, what are you doing!" he shouted as he spun out around the corner to the main road. "Raine!"

* * *

The best thing about a small town was that people loved to talk. They noticed things. And they told their stories.

"She was out at the bus station late last night."

"I thought it was a bit strange since I'd just seen her at Grace's party. Lovely party, didn't you think so?"

"Frank asked her about it, but she said she'd just gotten an urgent call about her mother. Took sick with no warnin' at all."

"Left on the four-thirty connection to Chicago. It was still dark out."

Ray talked into the cellular phone over the buzz of his electric razor and the hum of the tires against highway pavement doing well over the speed limit.

"I'm seventy miles outside of Chicago," he groaned. "You're just finding out now that she never made it that far?"

"I'm sorry, Ray. We're doing the best we can here. Go back to your aunt's and wait for my call. Let us take it from here."

Daniel Cort's frustration was showing.

"Sorry, Cort. No can do. I'm in this thing now. Just tell me what you've got."

"Close as we can tell, she got off the bus in Indianapolis and headed southeast to Louisville."

"What's she doing, going in circles?"

"Looks like she knows she's being tracked," Cort replied.

"All right," Ray yawned. "I'm heading back toward Louisville. Keep me posted, will you?"

Ray took the next exit and pulled into the Shell station.

"Fill 'er up," he growled as he spread the map out over the steering wheel and leaned into it.

"Check under the hood?"

"No," he mumbled. "No time."

* * *

Raine said a silent prayer that Ray would remember what she had said about heading into Chicago and making an effort to disappear. Once he'd checked with the locals in Walt Whitman, he would be led straight there. In the meantime, she had caught a bus out of Louisville and stopped just across the Tennessee border to connect to yet another lonesome town.

She would just keep on going, that was her plan. She would take one bus and then another. She would go as far away from Chicago as she could go on the little money that she had on her. Somewhere in the south perhaps. One of those sleepy little bayou towns would suit her nicely. Maybe she could even call upon that southern accent that had been lying dormant inside her since living in Louisiana as a child.

There were three hours to kill before the bus left, so Raine decided to wander across the highway to the truck stop for something to eat. She couldn't remember the last thing she'd had.

Oh, yes. Grace's birthday cake.

She slipped into a booth near the front and opened up the menu. She was so hungry that everything looked good to her, but she settled on a turkey sandwich and a green salad with ranch dressing.

"Anything to drink?" the waitress asked between chomps of peppermint gum.

"Lemonade."

Raine returned the friendly smile shot her way by the trucker seated up at the counter. His blue eyes were deep-set, and his skin was ruddy and splotchy. The plaid flannel shirt he wore was rolled up to the elbows, and his jeans looked as if he'd been in them for weeks on end.

"Long way from home, little lady?" he asked as he took a sloppy gulp from the cup of coffee in front of him.

"Not too far," she improvised with just a touch of the accent she hadn't called upon in years.

"Whereabouts ya headed?"

Great. The inquisitive type.

"Down south," she generalized. "How about you?"

"South, too. I got a load to drop down Baton Rouge way."

A ride as far as Baton Rouge. Shotgun in an eighteen-wheeler. That was just the surprise that might throw Ray and Harrison off the track, and it would keep some of that money in my pocket to boot.

She sized him up one more time. He looked safe enough. Some toddler's grandpa, no doubt.

"We're headed in the same direction then," she smiled with a glint of southern drawl. "Could I hitch a ride?"

The man looked at her curiously for a moment.

"I don't have much money. It's going to take everything I have to get a bus ticket. A ride would mean I might actually be able to eat a square meal or two on the way."

"Why not," he finally conceded. "It'll be nice to have the company."

Raine gobbled down her meal as quickly as she could, then ordered two oatmeal cookies to go.

"I just have a quick stop to make," she motioned toward the restrooms. "I'll meet you outside?"

"Sure enough," the old guy nodded, and she watched him head out the front door.

Once she had used the facilities, Raine paused in front of the payphone in the corridor. Quickly, before she could change her mind, she deposited a load of change into the phone and dialed. Her heart was pounding so hard that it echoed back at her through the receiver.

If Ray answered, she would just hang up.

"Hello?"

Grace's voice was stained with weariness and concern, and Raine knew that she was probably the cause.

"Grace?"

"Raine? Is that you, dear? Where are you, honey? Are you all right?"

"I'm fine," she replied, and she felt her hand trembling as tears rose to the surface of her eyes. "I'm sorry I left without saying anything to you. I just couldn't keep going without calling."

"Where are you going?"

"I . . . uh . . ." After a long pause and a deep gulp of air, she continued. "I can't tell you that, Grace. I can't tell anyone."

"Are you in some sort of trouble? Is there something I can do to help you?"

"You can't help me," she tried to chuckle. "I just wanted you to know how much I've appreciated the kindness you've shown me. You've been so wonderful, and I—"

"You've come to be like a daughter to me, dear. Please, let's try and work this thing out, whatever it is."

"I'm sorry, I can't," she blurted. "I love you very much, Grace. Thank you."

"Raine?"

Raine ended the connection gently and stared at the phone as if it were going to ring her back at any moment.

"I'm sorry, Grace," she whispered, then wiped the tears from her face as she made her way out the front door into the sunlight and placed a pair of sunglasses on the bridge of her nose.

"What's your name, anyway?" the trucker called to her as she climbed up into the cab.

"Lori." It was what came to mind. But a last name . . . He was sure to ask . . . She needed a last name!

"Okay, Lori. I'm Bill. You ready to roll?"

"Am I ever!"

Chapter Five

The further south they went, the more it reminded Raine of a home she had almost forgotten. Slidell, Louisiana. Not far from the party town of New Orleans, but far enough to have a small-town feel to it that New Orleans never had. Although they weren't heading far enough south to travel through Slidell, Raine did see a sign pointing in that direction.

"You gettin' hungry?" Bill asked her a few hours later, and she checked the digital clock on the dash. It read 6:30 P.M.

"A little, I suppose. I wouldn't mind stopping if you'd like to."

It had already become quite dark, and it was less than 10 miles down the road to the next truck stop, which was unusually quiet in comparison to the others they'd visited that day.

Bill ran into a couple of fellow truckers that were familiar to him and, following a quick bowl of clam chowder, Raine excused herself to take a nap in the truck while he had more coffee and tossed some darts.

"I'll be along in a bit," Bill called to her as she headed out, and she was glad for the time alone.

The bunk smelled of Bill, and it made Raine slightly nauseous. She had to lie on her back to escape the scent of him ingrained in the pillow. She was so tired that she didn't think to grumble about it. She was just happy to have a place to rest.

It wasn't long before she began to drift off, and it was as if she were gliding down a long, slippery slide into deep, warm waters. But waiting for her there was Ray, his face clear and sharp, his eyes accusing.

"Raine," he whispered to her, and he seemed to be reaching out for her hand at first, then he had her in his grasp.

"No," she called, but the word never made it out of her throat.

Sleep began to rise from her, like steam from a cold sidewalk, and she snapped open her eyes to find Bill leaning over her.

His smile was strange to her, and a sort of alarm began ringing inside of her as she blinked hard, wondering if she had just dreamed him there.

"What are you . . . doing . . ."

But Bill didn't answer. Instead, he just slid nearer to her, a questioning look in his eyes as he raised his hand and began to reach for her.

Raine didn't know what he had in mind, but she wasn't planning to stick around to find out. Suddenly, she curled up her fist and drew it back, slicing it through the air until it connected with the center of the old guy's gut.

Bill rolled back and began to writhe a bit, like a wounded cow, and Raine popped up from the bunk and crawled through the opening to the front seat. Snatching up her duffle bag from the floor, she leapt to the ground and took off at a full run across the dimly lit parking lot.

"Where you going?" she heard Bill screech from behind her, but she just kept on running into the darkness.

If she'd have been anywhere up north, she might have braved the cold and made a bed for herself overnight in the woods. But not in the south. The evening was balmy, and she could already hear the chirp of a hundred different kinds of insects that would descend upon a still, warm body in the grass in half a second's time.

She shivered with the thought of it. No, she would just keep on walking. She didn't even know where she was headed, but she didn't care. It was important to keep moving, she'd learned that for sure.

Her legs ached, and her back was convulsing almost non-stop now. How she yearned for a cup of Grace's English-blend herbal tea and the cradle of her four-poster featherbed.

She must have walked for hours along the deserted highway before she finally saw the yellow lights of the rest area. There would be vending machines there, and bathrooms.

The fluorescent lights flickered overhead, and it made Raine's vision seem unsure somehow. She splashed cool water over her face several times, and then lifted her shirt to investigate the source of intense pain that had been with her since early on after fleeing the truck stop.

Blood was caked all over her stomach and, as she washed it away, she found a nasty scrape about four inches long on the left side of her ribcage. She vaguely remembered scuffing the doorjamb of the truck when she'd run away, but she hadn't felt it since; she figured her skin was as numb as her mind.

"Oh, my!"

She hadn't known anyone was in the restroom with her, and she reeled to find a portly woman with coal-black hair standing behind her waiting her turn for the paper towels.

"That looks horrible," she cringed. "Does it hurt?"

"Yes," Raine nodded as she wrung warm water out over the gash.

"I have a first-aid kit in my car," the woman offered. "Let me go and get it for you."

"No, thank you. I'll be fine. I just need to get it cleaned up."

"Don't be silly. I'll be back in a flash."

The woman offered her name by way of introduction. "Carolyn Barney. From Montgomery, Alabama," then she set about cleansing the wound with an antiseptic wipe.

"Lori Martin," she said without thinking, and then groaned at her own carelessness. Of all the last names in the country, she had to borrow his at a moment's notice!

"Oh, I'm sorry. Did that hurt?" The woman obviously thought she was groaning in pain rather than aggravation.

"Just a little."

"Where are you from?"

"Slidell," she offered. "I'm on my way out west to visit some friends."

Suddenly the south had lost all its appeal.

"How did this happen?"

"I hitched a ride with a trucker heading my way. He got it into his head that I owed him a good time by way of fare."

"Oh, dear." The way she'd said it, Raine was reminded of Grace.

Carolyn seemed to know what she was doing, and she had Raine's wound clean and bandaged in no time at all.

"There we are," she sighed as she packaged up the first-aid kit properly. "You know, I'm heading to Oklahoma City. If that's anywhere near the direction you're headed, I would really love someone to talk to. I just hate traveling alone. My girlfriend, Esther, told me it wasn't safe these days, and I'm beginning to wonder if I didn't dismiss her too easily."

"I know what you mean," Raine nodded with a smile. "Oklahoma City would be just perfect for me."

The two women stopped at the vending machines and bought coffee and soda and a few things to munch on in the car, then headed over toward Carolyn's Buick in the lot. There weren't too many people around at that time of the night. A father and son walking their poodle near the picnic tables and a young girl perched on the hood of her car rocking a baby in her arms. Two elderly women were stretching next to a Chrysler that suited them, and a middle-aged man in wrinkled suit pants and a coffee-stained shirt looked out into the horizon as if he might find something of interest there.

As they passed him, the man looked curiously into Raine's eyes for only a moment, then snapped his gaze away and began to yawn. Raine flicked the lock on her door as Carolyn turned over the ignition and started out toward the highway.

"You can find a station, if you'd like," Carolyn offered, and Raine concentrated on turning the radio dial.

"Do you like oldies?" she asked the woman as she paused over an old Beatles tune.

"Honey, I *am* an oldie, or hadn't you noticed?"

Raine giggled as she turned up the volume. After a short time, she found herself carelessly singing along.

"She's been spotted, Ray. She's traveling west on Highway 20 toward Shreveport."

Michael Tyler was a young agent. Ray guessed he hadn't been on the job long, but his call confirmed that Cort had widened the inner circle to include Ray, and for that he was grateful.

"Louisiana!" he exclaimed. Where in the world was that girl headed?

"She was spotted in a rest area outside of Monroe. She picked up a ride with a female Caucasian, approximately fifty-five years of age. They're traveling in a blue Park Avenue. 1997 or 98. Alabama plates."

"If she was spotted, why didn't someone pick her up?"

"By the time it could be verified, she was already on her way."

"Shreveport is fairly close to the Texas border, isn't it, Tyler?" Ray asked hopefully.

"Yes, sir. We've notified Agents Ames and Farnsworth ahead of her in Dallas, We'll catch up to her. One way or another."

"This little lady's pretty determined." Ray half-smiled. "I wouldn't underestimate her ability."

"And don't underestimate ours, Ray. From what I've heard, you've been away from law enforcement for a long time. Have you ever interacted with the FBI?"

"In fact, I have," Ray stated casually.

"Maybe you've forgotten what we can do."

"Not at all, Mike. Put the word out to be careful with her. And get me the next flight to Dallas. I can pick it up at the Nashville airport within the hour."

"I'll see what I can do."

"Make it happen, Mike."

Ray closed the phone and tossed it to the seat beside him.

What had made Raine bolt the way she had? He couldn't help but wonder if he'd made some sort of mistake. He'd surely let his guard down lower than he'd ever done before, and he fought off the anger aimed at himself for letting her get to him the way she had.

A fleeting memory skipped across his mind just then, thoughts of his old friends back in San Diego, Sage and

Ben. Sage had been running from a past of her own when she and Ben had found one another. The difference being, of course, that they had carved out a happy ending for themselves. Ray wondered if such a thing was possible for he and Raine.

"Grace?" he sighed into the cellular. "Is everything all right?"

"Oh, Ray. I heard from Raine, dear."

"She called? What did she say?"

He hadn't thought she would take that chance in her effort to disappear. Once again, he'd let his guard down, and he hadn't counted on the strength of the bond between Raine and his aunt.

"Tyler? She phoned my aunt yesterday . . . Yes, place the tap, but I doubt she'll call again. It sounded as if she were saying her good-byes . . . Any word on my flight? . . . Good!"

They had stopped for the night in a town called Marshall, just across the Texas state line, when neither of them could keep their eyes open another moment. That morning, Carolyn suggested an early start on just a cup of coffee, then stopping for something to eat once Dallas was in clear sight.

The further on they pressed, the better, as far as Raine was concerned.

"We'll pick up 35 in Fort Worth," Raine said as she gave the map the once-over. "And that will take us north right into Oklahoma City."

"You're quite a navigator!" her new friend smiled. "I think I'll take you along on all my long trips."

"Sounds good to me."

From Oklahoma City, it was a straight shot over to Albuquerque. That looked good to Raine, and she traced the way on the map with her finger. No one would think to look for her that far west, especially after all the Chicago clues she'd left behind. But then she never would have figured on being found in Walt Whitman, Ohio, either.

"How about you take the car over and gas it up," Carolyn suggested, handing Raine a gasoline credit card, "and I'll go into the office and check out."

"I'll take a look under the hood too," Raine nodded, catching the keys the woman tossed her way. "See you in a few minutes."

Raine marveled at Carolyn. She'd handed over the keys to her car as if Raine was a longstanding member of the family. Her credit card too. Shaking her head, she made a mental note to warn her against doing that too often for fear of the woman getting burned by someone who wasn't quite as trustworthy as a frightened 135-pound renegade on the run.

"Help you?" the teenaged attendant asked as Raine climbed from the front seat of the car and handed him the credit card.

"I'm going to fill it, but I was wondering if you could check the pressure in the tires for us?"

"Sure, ma'am."

Ma'am. How old did he think she was?

She saw Carolyn making her way across the cracked pavement of the motel parking lot as she popped the hood and headed in for the oil dipstick.

"Lorraine Carmichael?"

Raine's head darted out from underneath the hood, and she spun on her heels to find two men in coordinating suits standing behind her. After a moment, she gathered her senses and forced out a laugh. "Nope. Sorry, fellas, you've got the wrong girl."

"Mrs. Carmichael, if you'll just come with us, we'd like to have a word with you. It will only take a moment."

"What's this all about?" Carolyn said sternly as she moved in on the situation.

"You wouldn't want your traveling companion involved, I take it," the taller one stated in a low voice.

Raine's heart pounded wildly in her chest, and her body hardened into stone. Carolyn was sure to get hurt if these were Harrison's men. They could turn forceful, and she wasn't about to let that happen.

"No, it's all right. They're friends of my husband's."

"You feel free to go along on your way, Miss. We'll see that she gets where she's going."

"Lori?"

A flush of embarrassment made its way slowly up Raine's entire body. She saw it coming, but could do nothing to stop it.

"Lori?" The tall, thin goon smirked.

"Your name isn't Lori Martin?"

She cringed slightly as the two men shared cocky grins.

"Come along, *Mrs. Martin.* Ray is doing just fine. He's on his way here as we speak."

"My bag," she said and nodded toward the car, and the short, silent one reached in the back seat to retrieve it.

"This it?"

"I travel light."

"Are you going to be all right?" Carolyn whispered as she took Raine's hand into hers.

"I'll be fine. Really," she lied. "You should be able to make Dallas in a couple of hours."

Carolyn tossed her arms around Raine and pulled her gently into her portly body. "I'll miss you."

"Thanks for everything."

Raine watched her walk away and sign for the gas before getting into the car. Carolyn cast her a look out the window as she drove away, and their eyes locked together until they could hold on no more.

"Come with us now?"

"Where are we going?" she asked as they confined her, one of them on each side as they headed back toward the motel.

Neither of them responded, and anxiety pressed down on Raine like a huge pack of cold mud. Icy fingers seemed to clamp tightly around her throat, and her thoughts were muddled and vague in ghostly outlines rather than solid forms.

As they opened the door to Room 114, it dawned on Raine that they had been there all along, having taken the room next door to her's and Carolyn's.

"Tell me, boys," she said mock-bravely. "Is Ray coming to take me back to Harrison, or is he going to just kill me here and be done with it?"

"I think you've got the wrong idea," the tall one began as he slid out of his suit jacket and flung it across the back of a chair. "My name is Ames. This is Farnsworth."

Introductions yet. Harrison hired himself a doozy of a team here. Nice to meet you. Coffee and cake, anyone?

Raine lowered herself into the chair in front of the chipped dresser and held onto the arms with a grip that turned her knuckles white. She had to get out of that room! But how?

"Listen, guys," she said softly. "I haven't eaten a thing since yesterday afternoon. I'm half-starved. I noticed a little coffee shop behind the gas station . . ."

Ames nodded at Farnsworth, and the man immediately turned and left the room, obedient as a trained dog.

"I was sort of hoping we could all go."

"Just stay where you are," Ames growled.

At least it was one-on-one now. She scanned the room carefully, hoping for a plan to jump out at her from somewhere. Anywhere.

Ames stood between her and the window, and the door was bolted shut. She strained to remember if the bathroom in her room the night before had had a window, but she didn't think it did.

Just in case . . . "Can I use the bathroom?"

He nodded her toward the facilities the way he had nodded Farnsworth out for breakfast.

Once inside the bathroom, she remembered how tiny hers had been. Nothing but walls, tub and toilet. No escape route at all. She considered just locking herself in, but that didn't hold out too much hope. Chances were these guys had guns and they'd just shoot the lock right off the door. They seemed like the type to do that.

The slam of the outside door sent a chill racing through her. It was too soon for Farnsworth to have brought back the food, and she assumed it must be Ray. She was terror-stricken at the thought of facing him again, and yet oddly anxious for it at the same time.

She swallowed the lump in her throat and took a deep breath before opening the door and stepping out into the room. Just as she did, a shot rang out, clear and ear piercing, and she screamed with it simultaneously, then watched in horror as Ames fell back on the bed like a rag.

Raine's eyes met those of the shooter, and she recognized him as Delaney, one of Harrison's key men. Shock struck her in the back of the neck and twanged like the string of a bow.

Delaney outstretched his hand, and she backed away from it, numb—as if from a drug.

"You've been a very bad girl, Lorraine."

"No," she whimpered. "Please."

"Just calm down."

At that moment, the door burst open and Delaney reeled toward it as Ray and Farnsworth exploded in at him.

Her eyes met Ray's for one stirring instant, and he yelled at her, "Get in the bathroom! Take cover!"

She was unprepared for her body's immediate, unquestioning obedience, and she backed into the bathroom and brought the door shut behind her. She sank to the commode like a long, light sheet of plastic, covering her ears and breathing in frantic, inconstant pants mingled with soft, uncontrollable whines.

Another shot rang out, and she could feel it down to her very soul. She was accosted by a quick flash of Ray falling back to the bed, a gaping hole where his chest used to be. Ames' body but Ray's face. That beautiful face, crumpled up as if it had been a painting left out in the rain.

Suddenly, the door whizzed open, and he was there. Alive and well. Standing before her that way, he seemed so large and valiant. All that was missing was the suit of armor.

"Raine," he said, then scooped her up like a load of laundry into his arms and held her there. "Raine." He repeated her name again and again, and it seemed to soothe him as much as it did her.

She wanted to kiss him but, from somewhere, she managed to find the self-control not to. She forced herself to remember that this man was not what he appeared to be. No matter how warm the embrace, he was a man to be feared, not loved, and Raine shoved her emotion for him down below the surface, silently soaking in his presence until she was saturated.

"Martin, you've got to get out of here," Farnsworth urged from the other room, but Ray was unwavering. "Too much attention, my man. Take her and blow while you still can."

Ray straightened. He seemed to feel that Farnsworth was right.

"Carmichael doesn't know about you, so they won't be looking for you. Now, go!"

"We've got to get out of here," Ray told her, looking her squarely in the eye and holding her up by the shoulders.

"Please, don't take me back. I can't go back."

"No, I won't," he promised as he led her through the motel room and out the front door. Her eyes locked on Ames as she passed him, and tears rose in her eyes and flooded down her cheeks in streams. She noticed Delaney in a heap on the floor in the corner, and she shuddered, forcing herself to look away.

"Yes, we need assistance," Farnsworth said into the phone as he frantically waved them on out the door.

A broken styrofoam plate flapped in the breeze in the center of the parking lot where Farnsworth had obviously dropped it upon hearing the first gunshot.

"In the car," Ray ordered, and she acquiesced without question.

"Martin!" They both turned toward the whisper, and Raine watched as Farnsworth, the phone still to his ear, tossed her duffle bag out the door into Ray's arms. "Good luck," he yelled to Raine, and then Ray quickly slid behind the wheel of the car and rolled out of the parking lot.

"Yes . . . Yes, I can be there in ten minutes . . . All right. See you then."

Raine watched him as Ray turned off the cellular and folded it into his pocket.

"They'll have a car for us a few miles up the road," he told her. "We'll have a bit of freedom at that point."

Freedom. That sounded pretty funny coming from him.

"Are you all right?"

She nodded without looking at him.

"Can I get you anything?"

"How about a cab?"

"That would be . . . *me*." He smiled. "Where would you like to go?"

Raine didn't have an answer. If the truth were known,

she was exactly where she wanted to be. With Ray. And that sickened her all the more.

"Are you hungry?"

She was starving, but she only admitted to, "A little."

"As soon as we make the change, we can stop for something to eat."

Raine nodded, then intently watched the scenery pass them by. When she couldn't stand it a second longer, she turned her entire body toward him and shouted, "Who are you? Tell me!"

Ray responded with a surprised laugh, and he reached over and smoothed the hair back away from her face. "Yes, I guess you are entitled to an explanation at this point, aren't you?"

"I'd say so," she replied without wavering. "Do you work for my husband?"

"God, no!" he said seriously, and then softened at her terrified expression. "No, baby. You're way off track."

"Then enlighten me." She was in no mood to be charmed. She just wanted the facts. And she wanted them fast.

"Let's make the switch and get some grub. Then I'll answer every question you have."

She nodded in agreement, and then turned back toward the scenery. Perhaps it would be better not to hear the truth on an empty stomach.

Chapter Six

Ray instructed Raine to stay in the car while he jumped out and exchanged pleasantries with an average-looking man with a balding head and a bit of a paunch. They had a quick, hushed conversation in which Ray's companion turned to look at Raine several times, then he slipped Ray a set of keys and was on his way.

"Take care, Ray!" he called as he hopped into the driver's seat of an old yellow van and took off.

Ray hurried back to the car, pulled Raine's duffle out of the back seat, then whispered, "Let's go."

Once they were tucked inside the white Miata left for them at the edge of the restaurant parking lot, a long-haired man in his mid-20s meandered out of the coffee shop with a toothpick in his mouth. The nod he sent Ray's way was barely detectable and, as they coasted out toward the main road, Raine watched the man slide into the car they had driven in, reach under the seat for the keys and quickly turn over the engine.

"This is some operation you have going here," she said once the restaurant was out of view. "Are you some sort of cop?"

81

Ray didn't answer, and Raine didn't pursue it. They just drove on in silence down the highway at a safe, respectable 60 miles per hour.

"Do you feel like a hamburger?"

"Sounds fine." She was so hungry that just about anything would have been fine with her.

"Four burgers with the works," Ray ordered at the drive-thru window of a hole-in-the-wall called Jake's. "And two chocolate shakes."

"Make mine vanilla."

"Make that one chocolate, one vanilla," he corrected, then drove up to pay the man who had taken the order.

Once they had the bags in hand, Ray rounded the corner and went down a couple of blocks, pulling into the parking lot of an abandoned building. Backing the car into a space drawn by long-faded yellow paint, he turned off the ignition and looked at Raine.

"You're a sight for sore eyes," he told her. "I was beginning to wonder if I was ever going to see you again."

Raine wordlessly doled out the food, adding straws and napkins to what she'd piled on Ray's leg. Her mouth was watering as she unwrapped the sandwich and took a big, messy bite.

"I don't work for Harrison Carmichael," he said matter-of-factly as he unwrapped his own burger.

"Then who do you work for?"

"The U.S. Government at the moment."

Raine's mouth froze solid in mid-bite.

"You eat." He grinned. "I'll explain."

The story was a long one, and she had finished both hamburgers and was skimming the straw along the bottom of her milkshake before it was over.

Raine's husband, Harrison, had been under surveillance by the FBI for a very long time. Two operatives had infiltrated his midst, working undercover as part of his team when one of them had been discovered. Carmichael had brought in four of his men to watch, one of them being the other operative, as he screwed a suppressor onto the shaft of a .32-caliber revolver, held it to Joe Dunne's head and pulled the trigger without even flinching. That night, as it happened, was the night that Lorraine Carmichael had expertly escaped, but she was spotted by the agents watching the compound. They'd been tailing her ever since.

"Is Grace really your aunt?" she asked, confused.

"Yes."

"But how did . . . you . . . know?"

"I didn't," he replied.

"Could you be a little less clear?"

"When the FBI tracked you to Grace, they went looking for something—"

"Or someone?"

"Or someone," he confirmed, "that would hook them into her."

"Why you?"

"That's what I've been asking myself since the day they arrived. I'm former law enforcement, and they have something I need. So they dangled it over my head like a carrot and enlisted my involvement. All they want from you is information."

"But I don't have any information," she told him tearfully. "I didn't know anything about Harrison killing Joe Dunne. I mean, I knew Joe, of course. But I didn't even know he was dead. What do we do now?"

"Well . . . the FBI, thinking you might have run off that night because you witnessed something that could pin Joe's murder to your husband, assumed they would be needing you alive when they built the case against your husband. They recruited me to keep an eye on you, maybe pick up some information along the way. They knew that, if they could find you, so could Carmichael eventually, and I was to protect you for as long as we could hide you. My plan is to keep on doing that."

"And can I ask . . . who was supposed to protect me from you?"

"I deserved that," he admitted. "I never counted on your sweeping me off my feet the way you did."

She didn't want to ask, but she had to know. "So that part was genuine?"

"Do you doubt that?"

"I don't know what I think right now," she replied, and a mist of emotion swept across her soul. "Except that you seem like my best bet for staying alive at the moment."

"Delaney was the hit man sent after you by Carmichael, and he has been taken out," he said, wiping the last of his meal from his mouth with a paper napkin, then depositing it into the paper bag sitting between them. "But Carmichael undoubtedly knows the vicinity where you were located. I think the best thing we could do is drive as far as Dallas and hole up somewhere there. To fly out would be too risky, too easy to trace. I thought we'd check into one of the finest hotels, order a lot of room service and wait them out."

"What does that mean? I mean, wait for what?"

"For instructions on what to do next. We'll want to change your appearance, and mine too, I suppose. And let the FBI handle things from there."

Raine shook her head. It was all so much to take in, and she was fast approaching overload.

"I know, baby," he said softly, as if he could read the thoughts even she couldn't pin down. When Ray reached over and caressed the top of her hand, electricity shot up her arm and straight to her heart. "The faster we get on the road, the faster you can find somewhere to lay your head."

"I'd like to call Grace when we get settled, if that's all right."

"We'll see," he vaguely replied. "Let's see how things go."

When they pulled up to the valet at The Four Seasons Hotel, Ray reached across Raine's lap and pulled a brown wallet from inside the otherwise-empty glove box.

"What's that?" she asked him.

"Identification." He opened it and took a quick look. "Making us Mr. and Mrs. Edmund Grainger." Raine was amazed. "If it weren't all so deadly serious," he added as he slid out from behind the wheel, "it might be a fun game, wouldn't you say?"

She smiled and shook her head as she stepped up to his side, then preceded him through the revolving glass door.

"Hang back in the lobby so no one gets a good look at you," he warned, then pulled a pair of wire glasses from his pocket and placed them on his nose. "My wife and I have reservations," she heard him say. "Grainger."

The lack of luggage was easily explained away by citing an airline mix-up, and Ray placed a firm arm around her and led her directly to the elevators once he'd acquired the key. When the doors slid open on the eighth floor, Ray reminded Raine a little of James Bond the way he poked out his head and looked in both directions before leading her into the hall.

Their suite was plush country fare splashed with minty greens and dusty roses. An overstuffed loveseat and a roomy wing-backed chair were flanked by an oblong coffee table near the window where sunlight poured over the whole grouping like rich maple syrup. A wet bar stood unobtrusively in the corner, paneled in thick, dark oak.

Raine stepped nearer the open door to the far side and peered through. Walls of dainty rows of flowers surrounded a queen-sized bed draped in a deep rose spread. Over top of it was a watercolor painting of a woman in a garden.

She ached to recline beneath it and dream of gardens and sunlight and floral scents, leaving behind the more sour essence of her current reality.

"Why don't you," Ray urged her as if he could read her every thought, and then he nodded toward the bed. "Get some rest."

"I don't know if I could sleep," she admitted. "As tired as I am, I'm doubtful."

"You need to relax. Why don't you soak in a hot tub first, and I'll order you a cup of tea. That should put you right in the mood."

Raine would have liked to have been stronger than that, but she didn't have it in her. She nodded in agreement, then headed straight through the bedroom for the creamy-yellow flowered bath. The tub was large and inviting, and she dumped the entire bottle of complimentary bubble bath into the steaming water. Shedding her clothes was a relief, and she left them in heaps wherever they fell on the pale yellow tile.

"A pot of tea." She could hear Ray clearly in the distance, once she'd turned off the spigot and climbed in. "Something herbal, if you have it . . . Good. And my wife takes cream and sweetener."

My wife. It had rolled off his tongue like silk. No forethought. No examination or effort. *My wife.* It brought the first smile to Raine's lips that she could remember since leaving Carolyn Barney. It had been so long, in fact, that she felt the pull of her smile muscles at both sides of her face.

Resonant melodies of Vivaldi danced through the suite, seeping gently underneath the door to stroke her nerves with tender fingertips until she was ready to rise from the water as if baptized, reborn. She lifted the smaller of the two white terry robes from the hook on the back of the door and wrapped herself snugly into it.

The Four Seasons crest was embroidered with shimmering thread on the breast pocket, and she ran her fingers gingerly over it. It was hard to believe that she was there with Ray. A hotel suite. Rising out of the bath and heading in to lounge on the sofa over a cup of creamed tea. Everything else seemed to slip away for moments, instants, beneath the shadow of it. And then they would come hurtling back at her like a softball through a plate glass window.

"Drink this," Ray invited as she strode into the living room. "Then see if you can get some rest. I'm going out for a bit to—"

"Going out?" she cried. "You're leaving me?"

"I'll only be a few minutes," he explained carefully. "I want to get some hair color and things. We have to think about changing our appearance somewhat."

"What about clothes?" she asked. "I don't have much of anything with me that would paint me as the other half of a couple that could afford to stay here."

"That's a thought." She watched him as he tapped his finger several times on the arm of the chair.

"I could go with you. I could tie my hair straight back from my face. And I noticed a rack of baseball caps in the gift shop downstairs."

"All right, then. I'll go and buy you one while you sip your tea. What's your favorite team?"

"I . . . don't know very much about baseball. What's yours?"

"Padres it is then. I'll be right back," he smiled, then pointed at the tray on the table in front of her. "Drink up."

Once he'd gone, Raine lifted the cup and saucer from the tray and carried it into the bedroom with her. Sitting down in front of the bureau, she pulled her hairbrush from the front pocket of her bag and began to run it through her thick nut-brown hair.

As an experiment, she brushed her bangs straight back

out of her eyes, leaving her forehead bare. It did indeed change the entire look of her face, and she nodded at her reflection. She would tuck them back beneath the hat Ray was to bring her.

Raine smoothed lotion on her legs and arms from the sample tray in the bathroom. Its scent wasn't nearly as pleasant as her usual, but she had left that far behind in Walt Whitman. She pulled a pair of denim jeans from the bag, followed by a black sweater and a pair of socks, then searched the two other compartments until she came across tennis shoes and pulled them out as well. She dug deep into the pocket of the jeans and located the black terry band she thought she remembered was there and set it aside to fasten a ponytail into place once Ray arrived with the hat.

Just about the time she was tying her shoes, Ray entered the living room and called out to her. "It's just me, darling. Your loving husband."

Raine let a little giggle escape, and looked up to find him standing in the doorway.

"The choices were grim," he pouted, producing a plain black cap with no insignia at all. "This is what we ended up with."

"Well, it's not a Padres hat," she teased, "but it will do."

When Raine emerged from the bathroom, her bangs pulled back beneath the hat and sunglasses covering her distinctive eyes, Ray did a double take.

"Excellent!" he congratulated her. "I wouldn't have known you on the street."

"Does that mean I don't have to color my hair?"

"You're not interested in finding out if blonds have more fun?"

"Not at all," she admitted. "I've never put a chemical of any kind on my hair, and I'm not enthused about starting now."

"It is a shame to cover up the perfect shade that God

gave you. Maybe you can just become the Mad Hatter for a short while."

"That would make you . . . Ray in Wonderland?"

Ray shook a finger at her with a grin, and then offered his arm. "Come, wifey."

"That's Mrs. Grainger to you." She sniffed, then took his arm and followed his lead to the door.

Ray sat back like some sort of royalty while she, his favorite from the harem, paraded by him in a fashion show of dresses, slacks, vests, jackets and, of course, hats. Thumbs up to that one, thumbs down to those. He seemed to be having the time of his life, and Raine had to admit that she was enjoying it as well, and took care to remind herself every so often that this was no game they were playing.

By the time they were through, Ray had to purchase a small suitcase to hold everything they had bought. He let Raine pick the one she liked best, a floral tapestry bag with gray leather trim.

"It's on Uncle Sam's tab," he said. "He's such a kind old guy."

"The first order of business when we get back to the hotel," Ray told her as she climbed into the Miata, "is to toss that sports bag you've been carrying in the nearest dumpster."

"I'd like to keep it," she told him, then responded to the question on his face. "This bag is beautiful, but it's large. I can't haul it around with me if I have to take off in a hurry."

"Sweetheart," he said, taking her face in his hands and staring hard into her eyes, "if I have anything to do with it, you're never going to have to take off like that again."

"But you can't be sure," she objected. "You don't know

what's going to happen. As long as Harrison is out there . . ."

"We're hoping he won't be out there much longer. We're planning to put him away for a very long time, Raine. I'm determined to take him down. More now than ever."

"Ray, you said they had something that you needed. Something they were dangling over you like a carrot. Can I ask what it is?"

"This isn't the place for this conversation," he replied after a long, silent moment. "How about some dinner?"

"Somewhere wonderful," she suggested hopefully, and Ray rounded the car and slid in beside her.

"Your wish is my command."

The restaurant was colorful and fun, all of the pine tables painted in bright colors, and upbeat mariachi music piped in from every corner. The waiter led the couple to a beautiful table on the veranda beneath a tall, leafy tree strung with white lights.

"It reminds me of that old barn of yours," Raine reminded him with a dreamy smile. "Remember? The night of Grace's party."

"I'll never forget that night."

"Do you think I'll ever see that house again? Or Grace, or the sleigh?"

"I can almost guarantee it," he whispered, taking her hand between both of his. "I'm willing to stake my life on it."

"Oh, Ray. Don't say that. Don't ever say that."

"We're not just playing Mousetrap here, darling," he said, rubbing the top of her hand gently with his thumb. "It's going to be a fight to the finish."

"Tell me what he's done, Ray. What has Harrison done to make the United States government interested enough to plant undercover agents?"

"For starters, he's implicated in more murders than just Joe's. He's what is known as a public enemy. That's someone considered to be very dangerous who is sought by many different law enforcement agencies for many different crimes."

Ray paused and smiled at the waitress as she poured ice water into their glasses. "Can I get you something from the bar?"

Her smile was just a fraction too broad, and Raine could tell that she was smiling for Ray alone.

"Oh, darling," Raine cooed for the young woman's benefit, "let's have something festive to celebrate our love. A pitcher of margaritas for my husband and I."

The word *husband* seemed to spark something in the girl, and her eyes darted immediately to Ray's left hand. No ring. She walked away without a word in return.

"You're wicked," he teased.

"Just careful," she returned. "Now please go on."

"They've collected a file filled with circumstantial evidence against Carmichael. He is very actively involved with an underground medicine man operating under the alias of Loomis."

"Glen Loomis," Raine nodded. "We've met on several occasions."

"Well Loomis' name is actually Linderman. He's somewhat of a political refugee from East Germany who specializes in plastic surgery. He and Carmichael have been involved in a huge scam operation wherein they smuggle some real questionable characters into the United States, perform a little facial magic on them, keep them underground until a new identity is established and then cycle them into the American way of life."

"You've got to be kidding," Raine sighed, and they both fell silent while the waitress poured their first round of drinks from the tall crystal pitcher.

"Are you ready to order?"

"You do the honors." Raine motioned to Ray, and he proceeded to point out the special for two, a sampler platter of cheese enchiladas, chili rellenos, a Mexican salad, and the standard rice and beans.

"There are other items," he continued without missing a beat, "such as collusion involving an estimated sixteen million in art forgery, some activity in a numbers racket and some petty stuff that doesn't concern us nearly as much as the conspiracy between Linderman and Carmichael."

"I knew about the art forgery." She nodded, taking a long sip from the stout glass of margaritas. "Or at least I suspected. But you know . . . I remember seeing some file folders with photographs and medical information in them. When I asked Harrison about it, he blew sky high. I wonder if those were files on the faces he's helped to change."

"And you're sure photographs were included?"

"Well, yes. Processing what I saw with what you're telling me . . . They were probably before and after shots, Ray. He keeps it all in the vault down in that hidden room of his . . . Do you know about the hidden room?"

"Yes," he replied thoughtfully. "That's why our man was killed. He was caught trying to gain access. If only we could get into that room and get our hands on those files. It would be more than enough to take Carmichael down permanently."

"I wish I'd known."

Ray stared Raine down for a long moment.

"Sweetheart. Do you know the code to the hidden room?"

"I should." She shrugged. "It's my birthday."

Ray grinned more broadly than she thought he was able.

"There's more to the hidden room than just the code," she told him worriedly. "There's a whole maze of rooms down there no one knows about except Harrison, Delaney—"

"Who's now dead."

"—Barringer and me."

Barringer was Carmichael's second in command. The only human being on earth who probably knew every secret Harrison had to conceal.

"Do you know how to work your way through the maze?" he asked carefully.

"Unless Harrison has changed all of the codes."

As the waitress laid out a feast before them, Ray leaned back in his chair and sighed, staring at Raine so hard that it tickled from the pit of her stomach straight up into her throat.

"And then what happened?"

"Well, he was apprehended at the Mexican border, heading down there to take care of Sage once and for all."

"Thank God he was caught!" Raine gasped, and then shook her head. "So where are Sage and Ben now?"

"Operating a home for orphaned kids in San Diego," he told her, placing his hand at the small of her back and leading her out the door. "Happily married with a whole brood they call their own."

"I love a happy ending," she said, and Ray took her hand into his and raised it, planting a kiss just above her center knuckle. He didn't tell her so, but Ray promised himself just then to create a happy ending she would be proud of. One where the boy and girl lived happily ever after. He wasn't entirely sure how to go about it, of course, but he was determined to make it happen just the same.

The night air was crisp, and Raine seemed to like it that way. Ray watched her as she closed her eyes and inhaled, taking it into her lungs as far as it would go.

"I had no idea it got so chilly in Dallas," she told him as he joined her on the curb.

"Yeah, it can get icy here during winter. Are you ready to go back to the hotel?"

"Yes." She nodded and timidly took his hand as he offered it. "Oh!" she cried suddenly, stopping in her tracks. "Ray, I forgot my sunglasses on the table."

"I'll go get them. You stay back near the lobby."

She walked back to the entrance with him and released his hand as he headed in the door.

"May I pull your car around for you, sir?" the valet asked.

"No, thanks. I parked in the lot."

"I wouldn't mind, just the same."

Ray thought it over a moment, and then nodded, tossing him the keys. "It's the white Miata down the last row."

He shot Raine a wink, then headed inside as the young boy ran off eagerly toward the parking lot. It took only moments for Ray to reappear, Raine's sunglasses in hand and an eager smile across his face.

"I ate way too much." He grinned, then patted his stomach.

Their smiles disintegrated, falling down their faces like shattered glass as time began to move in slow motion. A piercing blast drew all eyes toward the edge of the parking lot.

"Raine!" Ray called, and he looked up to see pure and certain terror wash over her in a riptide wave.

Splinters of glass careened through the air in a hundred different directions, and fire blasted 50 feet into the sky in thick, black billows.

"My God!" Raine screamed, and Ray's arms drew her to him, then over his body and down to the ground where he formed a cape over her like a pup tent. "Ray!!" she shouted, her face hard against the pavement. "Our car!"

Ray peered over his shoulder in horror at the site of the explosion, still smoothing his hand in repeated patterns across Raine's trembling back. Dozens of voices came together in the air around them. Women's screams and children's sobs.

"Call an ambulance," a man coughed.

"He's dead!" another squealed.

In every direction, automobiles were bent like broken toys, and black smoke rose from what was left of the smoldering Miata. Several employees of the restaurant struggled to put out a fire that was feeding off landscape near the street.

"Raine, get up," Ray whispered, and he pulled her by the arm to her feet.

"My God, Ray!" she sobbed, and buried her face into his chest.

"We've got to go, Raine. Now. Come on. Follow me . . . It's going to be all right. Just follow me."

Chapter Seven

It had been a long night. Ray had phoned in for backup assistance within moments of the car explosion, and it seemed like hours before someone finally showed up 40 minutes later to pick them up one block north of the Alpha Beta parking lot.

From there, they were taken directly to Love Field where a charter airplane flew them into Los Angeles. They were met there by two agents posing as an elderly couple and were handed the keys to the rental car they were to drive to San Diego.

In the six or seven hours they had been traveling, Raine would bet they hadn't spoken fifty words between them. She had held tightly to Ray's hand, and had even managed to doze off on the plane as she nuzzled her face into his chest and he held her tight with both arms.

It was nearly 2 A.M. when they stepped into the lobby of The Horton Grand Hotel in San Diego's gaslight district. Lush green trees were strewn with tiny white lights in the courtyard across from them, and a quick flash of homesickness for Walt Whitman washed over Raine. How she longed to see Grace again, sip tea with her and talk over things as inconsequential as the price of yellow squash, the latest shipment of books at The Bookmark or the coming winter season.

Ray deposited Raine on an antique couch upholstered in mauve velvet, at the opposite end of the lovely lobby. She watched him stride across to the registration desk like a man with a mission while dozens of birds in white iron cages sang out to him as he passed.

The man behind the old walnut desk was dressed in period costume, a tweed cap on his head and a starched white shirt and suspenders with short pants resembling knickers. The whole place had a warm, Victorian feeling to it, and Raine noticed that she was starting to feel muscles in her body relax for what felt like the first time in weeks.

"Room 210," she heard the man say, and she looked up in time to see Ray snatch up the card key and hurry back toward her. "Would you like help with your bags, Mr. Sommer?" the man called to him.

"No." He tried to smile without much luck. "Our bags will be sent over tomorrow. Is there a valet for the car?"

"Yes, sir. If you'll just leave your keys with me."

Ray handed him the keys as he took care to shield Raine from direct view.

"The elevators are through the doors and to the left," the man offered cheerfully, "or you can take the stairwell through the other doors."

"Thank you." Ray said as he led Raine through the doorway toward the elevators.

They crossed outside, and beyond a lovely white lattice barrier was the courtyard. Trees reached past the second floor of the hotel square, and white wrought iron tables and chairs dotted the brick floor. Twinkling lights and hurricane lamps brought dim illumination to the scene, and the night was so still that their footsteps echoed as they crossed.

Through another set of doors and left into the alcove. As

Ray rang for the elevator, Raine inspected the setting of furniture between the two cars. A large-seated Chippendale chair from the 18th century placed casually next to a round mahogany table covered in lace. A gold girandole mirror hung on the wall behind it, and Raine noticed for the first time how weary and drawn she and Ray both looked. They were like strangers in the reflection, worn and completely spent.

She wordlessly stared out the glass of the elevator as the courtyard moved further and further away. A maze of hallways finally led them to Room 210, and Ray poked the plastic card into the slot and flipped the brass door handle.

Even at this level of exhaustion, the designer in her could appreciate the room for what it was. Exquisite. Thick rose carpet invited bare feet, and rich floral bedspreads covered two identical beds which were tall and overstuffed. Fabric was draped along the wall over each of them in a lacy Victorian valance, and each bed was topped with huge, glutted pillows.

Brass hurricane lamps protruded from the walls on the far side of either bed, and Ray pulled the chain on one of them to add soft, yellow light to the room. Huge lace-sheathed windows stood behind a delicate table and an inviting mauve chair framed in decorative walnut carvings.

Ray flicked a switch on the wall that brought the hiss of a gas flame up into the rose marble fireplace while Raine pressed open the dainty French door which led to a small balcony overlooking the courtyard below. She reentered the room to find Ray perched on the bed nearest the door, his shoes off and his feet carelessly crossed at the ankles.

"Yes," he spoke into the telephone. "Yes. And some clothes. Everything we bought was in the car. We're left only with what we have on our backs. I told the hotel clerk that our luggage would be sent over tomorrow, so you can play it that way."

Raine was too weary to think about details. She'd leave that to Ray, she decided, and crossed the room, running a finger along the mirrored armoire much like the one that had stood in her own bedroom in Walt Whitman as she headed into the bathroom.

"She's a size 6," he told whomever was on the other end of the line, and she smiled at the fact that he'd remembered. "About five-foot-five . . . Shoe size?"

"Six and a half," she called back before closing the door behind her.

"Six and a half," she heard him repeat. "I can't tell you how much I appreciate this, Ben. I didn't know who else to call."

Raine ran cold water into the basin, cupping some in her hands and splashing it across her face. She noticed the brass pipe that led up from the toilet and pulled the chain fastened there, flushing the bowl with fresh water. A small cabinet on the wall displayed an array of lotions, bath foam and shampoo, and the lace shower curtain was tied back to reveal a large cream-colored tub. She removed one of the two crystal glasses from the cabinet shelf, ran cold water into it and took a long drink.

"Yes, all right," Ray was closing as she returned to the room. "We'll expect Sage in the morning then. It will be great to see her again."

"Expecting who?" she asked as he replaced the receiver to its cradle.

"Old friends," he said as he stretched out across the bed. "Sage Travis. I told you about her and Ben the other night. They ran a mission down in Mexico for a while, now an orphanage here in the city. Ben's up in Los Angeles at the moment, but Sage is going to bring us supplies to turn ourselves into different people."

"My hair?"

"Afraid so," he acknowledged. "Sorry, but we have no choice. The more changes we can make, the better."

"I understand." She timidly sat down on a diminutive corner of the bed he had chosen.

"Come here," he offered, and she practically dove into the arms that were outstretched before her. "We're going to be all right," he reassured her, then lowered his mouth over hers to seal the promise.

"I'm so tired," she told him once their mouths had drifted slowly apart.

"I know," he whispered, his eyes still closed from their kiss. "You'll rest tonight. And, Raine. I'll do everything I have to do to keep you safe."

His muscular arms drew her into him, and they lay there like that, front-to-front, arms locked around each other, for nearly 10 minutes without speaking another word.

"I'm going to get a shower," he finally said, and he kissed her long and deep before rising from the bed.

He stood over her for a long moment, caressing her hand and looking down into her eyes. But then he turned away, reluctantly it seemed, closing the bathroom door behind him.

Raine padded across the spongy carpet to the door, flicking the second lock into place before heading back over to the bed by the window. She listened intently to the spray of water in the next room. Her eyes closed, she pulled off her jeans and pressed them neatly across the back of the chair, then sighed before she took a step toward the window and pulled down the shades, one after the other, then unhooked her bra and pulled it from beneath the sweater. It was all she had to sleep in—a sweater and panties.

With a short stretch, she unfastened all but two of the buttons down the front of the sweater and crawled into bed. It was even softer than it had looked. Sleep found her at nearly the same moment that her head found the pillow.

* * *

Raine awoke to soft, gentle chords of classical music which seemed to be dancing on the air from somewhere in the distance. She blinked several times before the room came into focus, and she noticed that the French door was propped slightly open, and the music was wafting her way from the courtyard below.

A thousand small birds chattered their good mornings and the scent of freshly brewed tea made its way to her senses. She looked around the room and found that a porcelain pot and two cups were waiting on a tray at the table by the window along with a wicker basket filled with pastries, muffins and croissants.

Hushed voices drew her attention to the other side of the room. Ray's bed had been hurriedly straightened and a cloth tapestry suitcase lay open at the foot of it.

"Oh, good, you're awake."

Raine looked up to find Ray standing in the corner looking back at her. At least she thought it was Ray.

His shiny black hair was combed away from his face to expose perfect, sparkling eyes beneath small, round wire glasses. A neat beard and moustache were in place on his face, hiding that lovely cleft in his chin, and a small amount of gray splattered his jaw line and temples.

"Ray?"

"What do you think?"

She noticed a certain glint in his eye, an excitement that reminded Raine of a child showing off some wonderful thing he'd done in class.

"I wouldn't have recognized you," she admitted. Only here in their shared hotel room did she distinguish that long, muscular frame.

The clothes were new too. Black sweats and Nikes. And she looked to the open suitcase automatically, hoping there was something in there for her.

"Sage," Ray called toward the bathroom. "Come on out here for a moment."

Raine pulled the blankets up around her and remembered suddenly how almost naked she was beneath them.

"Hello."

"Raine, this is Sage Travis," Ray motioned to the stunningly beautiful woman with long fire-red curls.

"I'm sorry," the woman said as she sat down on the edge of the bed, "did we wake you?"

"No," Raine replied. "Did you do this to him?"

"Yes. How do you like a man with a beard?"

"I've always loved a little hair on a man's face." She grinned, and Ray self-consciously stroked the hair glued to his jaw. She didn't add that she missed that beautiful dimple which was now deliberately hidden. When it was all over, she would be anxious to remove the camouflage.

When it was all over. A chill ran up Raine's spine and tickled the hair at the back of her neck. Where would it all end? Would it ever end?

"Your turn," Sage said with a smack of her hands. "Ray, you scram for a couple of hours. When you return, your friend will be a new woman."

"I kind of liked the old one," he said softly as he plucked the card key to the room from the mantle, then called back to them as he slipped out the door. "Have fun, girls."

"Would you like a cup of that tea before we get started?" Sage offered kindly. "Want to wake up a little bit?"

"Yes," Raine replied, and pulled herself from the bed, careful to keep a sheet wrapped around her lower body.

Buttoning up the front of her sweater, she padded across the floor to her jeans and slipped them on.

Sage chatted about everything from her growing family of children at the orphanage to the minister who had somehow stolen her heart as they sipped tea and downed several items from the assortment in the basket, but Raine remained controlled and quiet, not sure how much Ray had told this woman about her or how much she would want her to know.

"Ray said you were old friends of his," Raine said timidly. "You and your husband."

"Ben," Sage said. "Ray was a police officer back then, and I was in a heap of trouble myself. Not unlike you, with someone I once thought I loved chasing after me."

So she knows the whole story then.

"If it weren't for Ray, I don't know where I'd be now. Dead, maybe. Aside from Ben, I can't think of anyone else I'd trust with my life."

Raine glanced up and looked at Sage cautiously. The woman's eyes were like emeralds, and they glistened at her as she smiled and took Raine's hand delicately into her own.

"Look," she said softly, and with a kindness that pinched slightly at Raine's heart. "I don't know everything about what you're facing, but here's what I do know for certain. You can trust Ray. He's one of those people you hope to meet in life, and he's going to see you through this."

Raine sighed, and then returned the smile.

"So, are you ready to change your look?" she asked with a grin.

"Not at all," Raine admitted, setting down her cup. "What are your plans for my hair?"

"Ray explained to me your reluctance to change it, so I think I have the next best thing!"

With a spring to her step, Sage hopped from the bed and hurried toward the front door, producing a large black case and spreading it open on Raine's bed.

Inside were vials and bottles and cases in various colors and styles. Sage lifted the top compartment to reveal several dozen more just like them. Lifting yet another section,

Raine gasped as she looked in. Several wigs were spread across the bottom like grass inside an Easter basket.

"Part of our ministry," she said with a nod. "Dramatic arts classes for the kids in the summer. We put on a play at the community theater at the end of every season."

As Sage pulled out the wigs, Raine inspected each one in amazement. A short pixie haircut, black as coal like Ray's hair color. Another was made of long spiral curls of fire-red that was much like Sage's natural curls, and yet another was a shoulder-length bob of straight, silky blond hair.

"Let's see which one suits you," Sage said, seemingly more to herself than to Raine.

She held each one of them up next to Raine's face and looked hard at her before going on to the next one.

"I don't have to cut or color my hair," Raine said. "I hadn't thought of a wig."

"You don't look bad as a blond," Sage said as she sized Raine up once more. "And the red would look fabulous with your fair skin. But the black brings on a sort of creepy quality. I wouldn't go with that one if I were you."

"I've always wondered what it would be like to be a redhead," Raine said, biting her lower lip as she lifted the curls to her face. "It sure looks magnificent on you!"

"Red it is, then!" Sage cried happily. "We'll be like sisters."

Sage led Raine to the chair and began to run a brush through her hair, pulling it rather roughly into a knot at the back of her head.

"Do you wear glasses?"

"No."

"Contacts either?"

"Nope."

"Any skin allergies I should know about? To makeup or eye products?"

"None that I know of."

And that's the way the conversation went from then on. The dazzling woman who had managed to down two blueberry muffins and a croissant, who loved a minister and ran an orphanage in her spare time, became suddenly serious and all business.

She wanted to ask Sage more about Ray's past, about his life as a cop and whether there had been a woman in his life back then. But she didn't. She determined to talk to him about it someday soon, though.

She wanted to know everything there was to know about Raymond Martin . . . about why he'd become a cop to begin with, and what it was in a person that led them to a life of knowing who to contact when you need a car, or what to do when that car blows up. Ray had seemingly known exactly what to do every step of the way in a journey that had no order or reason at all to Raine. Nothing appeared to surprise Ray. And yet every moment of this nightmarish adventure astounded Raine to her very core.

Looking at her reflection in the mirror brought about another surprise. Sage had transformed Raine into a completely different person with just a wig and some makeup. She had expected a somewhat trashy look to accompany the fire-red curls, but she looked like a sort of college coed to contrast Ray's new rather professorial appearance.

Tiny, subtle painted freckles dotted her nose and cheeks, and a bit of reddish pencil changed the entire shape of her eyebrows. Brown powder on her lids and a deep russet stain on her full lips completed the altered look.

"You're awfully quiet." Sage finally broke the silence.

"I look so . . . different."

"Wasn't that the objective?"

So it was. With that reminder, Raine nodded. "Yes. You've done a great job."

"The freckles will stay in place for several days, even if

you wash your face," she explained. "But in case you need them a bit longer, I'll leave the marker with you." She handed Raine a plastic case that zipped along the top. "Everything I've used is here. If you were paying attention, you shouldn't have too much trouble duplicating it. I'll take a Polaroid shot for you to hang on to and reference if you need to. It will be just like playing a part in a play."

Sage produced a camera from the large black case and snapped it. In a few moments, the image of someone Raine didn't even know emerged in the photograph. Someone with long red curls and high, arched brows.

Raine chose a pair of frames from a brown leather bag and set them into place atop her nose. She stared at her reflection for a long moment before busting out with laughter.

"This is unbelievable!"

"There are clothes in the suitcase on the bed for both you and Ray. He said he has new identification on him, and yours is in the zipper pocket on the inside of the case. I think your new name is Margaret Sommer."

"Margaret," Raine repeated, then crinkled her nose.

"You can always call yourself Meg," she suggested.

"Meg Sommer." That seemed better.

"Ray is your husband, David."

Raine remembered the man at the front desk calling Ray "Mr. Sommer." It amazed her how well organized it all was with such little notice. It made her feel safer, and a breeze of security washed over her like a blanket of sunshine.

"You'd better find something to wear."

The snap of the key in the lock a few minutes later drew their attention to the door, and Ray stepped inside and shut it tight behind him.

When his gaze fell upon Raine, sitting gracefully on the bed, draped in the floral cotton dress with cap sleeves and a rounded scoop of a neckline she'd chosen from the suitcase, he sighed.

"And who is this vision?"

Raine giggled, then turned away long enough to slide her feet into flat tan shoes. When she looked back, Ray was still wordlessly watching her, and she felt it as he drank her in like a glass of lemonade on a hot July afternoon.

"David, darling," she teased. "What have you been doing to occupy your time?"

"Well, Margaret," he returned thoughtfully, and she interrupted him with a smack on his hand.

"Meg," Sage corrected. "We don't like Margaret."

"Okay, Meggie." He grinned. "I've been wandering around the hotel."

"Casing the joint, huh?" she asked.

"Just checking out all our options."

"You're a natural," Sage chimed in as she closed up her black case and lifted it to her side. "Never an option left unchecked."

Ray smiled warmly at Sage, then gathered her into his arms and kissed her repeatedly on top of the head.

"I don't know what we would have done without you, Sage," he groaned as he enclosed her in a bear hug.

"Glad to help." She beamed at him as she opened the door. "We've been in your debt for a very long time. It's nice to be able to pay it back a little. But I wish you'd just come out to the house and stay."

"You've got to think of the kids first," Ray reminded her. "We can't put them in danger. Or you and Ben, either."

Sage looked as if she were about to cry as she slid her arms around Ben's neck and kissed him firmly on the cheek.

"Give my love to the kids. And tell Ben I'll call when I can."

"If you two need anything . . . *and I mean anything* . . . you call us. Okay? Promise me."

"I promise."

"Nice to meet you, Mrs. Sommer," she called back to Raine, and then shot her a wink before disappearing into the hall.

"I really like her," Raine said, and Ray nodded in agreement.

"I do too. She's a gem."

"Well," she sighed as she looked at the open suitcase, "should we unpack?"

"I don't think so. We should always be ready to go. We can just stand the case up inside the armoire and work out of it from there."

"Okay," she replied, but when she rose to do it, Ray beat her to it and had it in place before she even reached him.

"They serve English high tea down in the bar in about half an hour," he suggested. "I thought that sounded like something that might appeal to you. Would you like to go?"

"Can we?" she asked carefully.

"We're not on vacation, granted," he explained. "But we're not prisoners either. With our new looks, it should be safe."

A surge of joy splintered through her, and Raine grinned from ear to ear.

Ray held Raine's hand as he led her around the third floor of the hotel, pointing out this piece of furniture or that painting on the wall, then he stepped behind her to descend the stairs to the second floor where even more beautiful settings awaited them.

"This staircase is incredible," she commented as they made their way down. "It's got to be a hundred years old, at least."

As they advanced down the last set of stairs to the first

floor, Raine noticed that the bar she'd seen upon their arrival the night before had been transformed into a lovely tea room with white linen tablecloths and delicate china set up on each of the tables.

She noticed a place card on the table nearest the staircase marked with the words, SOMMER. PARTY OF TWO.

"That's us?" she asked enthusiastically.

"I made a reservation."

Ray held her pink tapestry chair for her, and then sat down across from her in one of his own. The huge windows behind him were draped in velvet, and the panels at the top were capped in gathers of white lace tied in the center with a knot. Enormous Victorian paintings graced the walls along with old framed black-and-white photographs of days gone by. There was so much to see that Raine had a hard time focusing in on one item at a time.

A gentile Englishwoman in a fancy white apron appeared at their table and presented them with menus from which to choose. There was Victorian tea, and then there was high tea, and Raine was pleased when Ray ordered the latter for them both.

"We have a selection of teas," the woman offered, but Ray stopped her by requesting English Breakfast.

"Very good, sir." The woman nodded and then headed off to the kitchen.

Classical music waltzed about them, soaring to the rafters of the 30-foot ceilings, then spilling down to dance throughout the room and across their spirits with the tender step of ballerinas in flight. The sterling pot of tea was preceded by its fragrant proclamation, and the server poured the first two cups.

Just the way Grace made it. Strong and rich. Raine added a splash of cream and two cubes of sugar. The first sip was like heaven. All that was missing was the company of Grace and the old kitchen table back in Walt Whitman.

Raine observed Ray closely as he watched the server present plates of edibles which included finger sandwiches of cucumbers, curried chicken and smoked salmon as well as Scotch eggs, and a flaky pastry wrapped around succulent spicy sausage. Two crystal glasses of sherry were added to the feast.

"If I can get you anything at all, just give me a wee nod," the woman offered, then hurried back toward the kitchen once again.

Every item tasted more wonderful than the last, and the twosome seemed to lose themselves together within the meal, sharing bites of this or that as they went along.

"Oh, Ray," Raine whispered, "I've just had the most wonderful thought! Wouldn't it be perfect to add a tea room to the plans for converting your family home to a bed and breakfast?"

Ray looked at her thoughtfully for a long moment, and then managed to summon a smile.

"What?" she paused. "You don't think we're ever getting back that far, do you? Will we ever make it through this crisis and go home to Walt Whitman?" Tears formed in her eyes and fell in droplets down her face as she leaned back in her chair and twisted the cloth napkin between her hands. "Will I see Grace again, Ray?"

"Of course you will," he assured her with a sigh. "We're going to get through this. I promise you."

"Then what was that on your face when I mentioned the bed and breakfast?"

"It was nothing."

She knew better. "Ray, please. What were you thinking just then?"

"I . . . was thinking how good it was to hear you say that you intended to return to Walt Whitman when this was over. And I was thinking that . . . your being there gave me a bit of extra incentive to return myself."

Raine's eyes grew wide, and they seemed to lock with Ray's. The thought of going home to Walt Whitman seemed to evoke a whole mixture of emotions in Ray that he wasn't willing to speak out. She'd seen a certain panic in his eyes and yet, at the same time, a silent yearning. A desire to escape the memories of the past, to never return again, stirred directly into the opposing emotions which had been brought to the surface by spending time there because of her.

"I shouldn't be trying to think that far ahead," she murmured. "One day at a time. It's just that it helps me find some hope to cling to. Do you know what I mean?"

"I'll be your hope for the moment," he replied as he leaned in toward her. "Cling to me."

Heat rose from the depths of her physical senses, and Raine felt a shudder of longing slip through every vein and every artery. There was nothing she wanted more just then than to cling to Ray and never let go.

"More tea?" the server asked as she stepped up between them.

"N-no, thank you."

Chapter Eight

Room service brought a light supper tray of pasta and vegetables, salads and rolls and a pitcher of iced water. Every bite was delightful.

Raine felt the huge bathtub with the lace curtains begin to call to her when she was through, and she excused herself to go in and indulge.

"I'll just watch the news," Ray told her, and she looked around the room in surprise.

"We have a television?"

With a grin, Ray pulled open the gold cabinet on the wall over the mantle to reveal a portable television inside.

"This place is adorable," Raine said as she removed the wig and hung it on the knob of the armoire, shaking her hair free as she wandered in to run a bath.

Ray watched her as she moved into the next room, and didn't release his gaze until the door had shut tight behind her. He restlessly switched the channels around the dial several times before finally landing on the local news. Two stories went by before he was able to tune out the splash of warm water in the next room and concentrate on what was being said. A local robbery. Two killed.

112

The scent of her wafted beneath the closed door and seemed to know just where to find him. He tried to occupy his mind with the details of their next move, but she was almost too much for him. The sweet, gentle fragrance of her seemed to wrestle him to the ground.

He never should have brought her to The Horton Grand! The place had romance piped in through the water. The walls dripped with it, the air was glazed with it and the beds invited it. What could he have been thinking?

A knock at the door drew his attention, and he was thankful.

"Yes?"

"Room service, sir. Take your table?"

Ray flicked open the locks. The waiter was wearing the same uniform the other one had worn, so he stepped back to let him come inside.

"Did you enjoy your dinner?"

"As always," Ray said.

"Do you come to the Horton often then?"

Ray started to reply, then paused to glance in the direction of a sudden splash of water from the bathroom. When he looked back again, the waiter was staring hard at him, so serious that it set him on edge, and his heart rose up inside his chest when he noticed the small handgun aimed directly at his mid-section.

"What's this all about?"

"That's enough," the waiter seemed to chuckle. "Not a sound."

"What do you want?"

"I said not a sound, Martin!" he spat, then nudged him toward the bed with the barrel of the gun, and Ray sat down.

Calling him by name must have meant that this was one of Carmichael's men. But how had they been found so quickly?

"I feel like something warm," Raine called from the next room. "Will you order a pot of tea?"

Ray looked carefully at the man in the waiter's uniform and their eyes seemed to lock, each of them in their own form of panic.

"Ray?"

"Answer her," he mouthed.

"I'll call right now," Ray replied softly.

His pulse was beating so hard inside him that he could hardly think over the noise of it. He had to act fast. She was going to step out of that bathroom at any moment, and he couldn't take a chance on her getting hurt.

"Let's step outside," he suggested quietly. "Talk this over like men. Leave her out of it."

"She's in it, old man," the phony waiter growled. "She's in it up to her eyeballs. And you and I both know I'm not leaving this room without her."

Ray looked away, shaking his head, then suddenly lurched from the bed toward the gunman. The gun went off once as he reached him, a tinny pop as the bullet passed through a small custom-made silencer attached to the end of the barrel. Ray was thankful he wasn't hit.

"Ray? Oh my God!"

He couldn't take even a moment to look back at her. He just pounded at the man with his fist, one blow after another after another, pounding his hand to the ground by the wrist all the while until the gun fell free from his grip.

"How did you find out where we were?" he demanded. "Tell me."

But the man just looked up at him with a queer half of a smile that fanned the flame of Ray's fury all the more. Holding him to the ground by the throat with both hands, Ray turned toward Raine who had backed herself up against the armoire.

"Is this one of his men?"

"Yes," she managed, and he could hardly hear her. "Coleman."

"I'm flattered you remember me, Lorraine."

"Don't even speak her name," Ray snarled, then banged Coleman's head one time against the floor. "Don't talk to her. Don't even look at her. Now, how did you know where to find us?"

The man was unwavering. He looked Ray right in the eyes without flinching. He wasn't about to talk, and Ray worked hard to bridle the rage that was rising inside of him.

"Get up!" he barked, then pulled the man up by the collar. "Now sit down! Over there."

Coleman fell into the chair by the balcony door, and Ray watched him cautiously as he bent to pick up the man's gun. He aimed it steadily at his forehead.

"Open the suitcase," he told Raine without looking back at her. "Pull out something long that we can tie his hands with."

In only a moment, she appeared at his side, the cotton belt to her new bathrobe extended toward him. "How's this?"

"Perfect. Do you know how to fire a gun?"

"Yes," she said, and he suspected that she was lying for Coleman's benefit.

"Hold this on him," he told her as he cocked it. "If he flinches, pull the trigger."

As he moved around behind Coleman, Ray looked at Raine for the first time. She looked surprisingly assured to him and, as inappropriate as the moment was for him to notice, he also thought she looked alarmingly sexy. The bathrobe had fallen open once she'd pulled away the belt, and the tiniest hint of lace could be seen. Her hair was down into her face and her eyes seemed to be on fire as she stared Coleman down, the gun aimed unquestioningly toward him.

This was a new side to her that he was seeing. There wasn't even a hint of panic in those eyes that remained coolly steadfast on Coleman. The rather innocent girl he had come to know was nowhere in that room, leaving in her place a woman who would undoubtedly do whatever she had to do, even if that meant holding a gun to the head of someone like Coleman and possibly pulling the trigger. There was a glint of quiet desperation in her steely gaze, and Ray was moved by it.

After he had tied the man's hands and feet to the chair, he took the gun from Raine and nodded toward the door. "Get dressed."

She didn't utter a word of question, only moved to the armoire and pulled out a pair of jeans and a sweater, and then plucked up the red wig on her way. She didn't even close the bathroom door before slipping out of the robe and into her clothes, and Ray had to force his gaze back to Coleman once he noticed her in the mirror's reflection. When he did, it was evident that Coleman had witnessed the exchange, and a creepy smile slithered across the man's face.

"Can't blame you, old man," Coleman jeered. "She's quite a looker."

Ray forced himself to ignore the man, pulling the suitcase from the armoire, and he zipped it shut with one hand while the other remained solidly firm around the cold handle of the gun. He hurriedly snatched up a washcloth from the wood cabinet around the corner, and then stuffed it fully into Coleman's mouth. One yank brought the phone wire straight out of the wall, and he plucked up the plastic key from the mantle before he backed toward Raine and led her with him out the door.

"The stairs," she pointed out, and Ray slid the gun into his pocket as they hurried down and through the lobby.

"Room 210," he told the valet.

"Are you checking out?"

"No," he lied. "Just visiting some family overnight. And we're terribly late. Can we get our car?"

Raine and Ray stood on that curb hand-in-hand, in total silence. Ray could feel her fingers twitching slightly in his grasp, and he noticed that her foot was tapping slightly on the pavement. Ray knew that her thoughts were in perfect alignment with his: They had to get out of there!

It was less than five minutes before their car came sleekly up to the curb, but it felt like an eternity to Ray. Tossing the suitcase over the seat into the back, he watched Raine slip into the passenger seat, and the valet slapped the door shut behind her. Once he was behind the wheel, he let out a sigh of relief and squealed away from the Horton Grand Hotel with more than one glance into the rear view mirror.

"No way, Cort! No way," Ray insisted. "We're on our own out of here. That's the way it has to be. You've got a leak somewhere, and I'm not going to put her life in your hands knowing that."

The conversation had gone round and round like that for nearly 15 minutes, and Raine stood silently beside Ray as he raged into the phone at some faceless representative of the United States government he seemed to know quite well.

"Not until you locate the problem," he said. "Once that happens, then I'll let you in on our plans. Until then, we're on our own ... What are you gonna do, Cort? Fire me? Please, do. I only wish you'd have done it before this ... Yes. I'll keep in touch ... I said I'll be in touch!"

Raine recognized a great deal of restraint in him as Ray

placed the receiver back to the hook of the payphone, then stood silent and still for several long moments.

"Let's go," he said finally, and she wordlessly followed him out the door of the coffee shop and back to the car. "We'll go to my office," he told her as he peeled out of the parking lot. "I'll get things going from there."

"Your office? You live in San Diego?"

"La Jolla," he replied. "We should be safe there at least until morning."

So many questions bounced around inside her head, but Raine didn't ask them. She leaned back into the seat and stared out the window, feeling oddly like a little girl being driven somewhere by her angry father. She didn't recognize Ray just then through the cloud of annoyance that hung over him, and she tingled with intimidation, yet she didn't know quite why.

"Ray?" she asked finally, and she was relieved at his kind gaze.

"Everything's going to be all right," he smiled reassuringly, and he slipped his large hand over her smaller one on the seat between them. That one insignificant gesture rinsed away all traces of the fear and doubt that had been so thick around her just a moment before.

Raine sighed, and a slick smile made its way across her face before she was even aware of it. She looked out the window as they hit the interstate, and the ocean glimmered beneath the lights like meteors streaming in the sky. As she observed him, Raine thought he could have driven this road in his sleep, and she was eager to see where it ended.

"Home sweet home," Ray seemed to whisper, and Raine watched him climb out and round the car to open her door. "Let's go."

She followed close behind him as he made his way down an alley toward one in a line of back doors.

"It's not much," he told her almost apologetically as he

peeled away the facial hair still glued to his face. "Especially for a lady like you. But it's safer than the houseboat."

"Houseboat?"

"Where I live."

Ray opened the door marked with peeling letters that read RAYMOND MARTIN. PRIVATE INVESTIGATOR, flicked the switch and flooded the room with flickering fluorescent light. Raine held back a gasp. She never could have imagined Ray in a place like this!

The steel-box desk was littered with scraps of paper, file folders and overturned beer bottles, and the trashcan beside it looked like a bonfire waiting to be lit. The tattered leather sofa angled into the corner displayed a heap resembling a woolen blanket and a tweed pillow in need of mending. The windows surely hadn't been washed in six months or more, and the pages of the desk calendar hadn't been turned in just as long.

"Are you shocked?" he asked, and she couldn't tell if he was amused or embarrassed. Maybe both.

"A little," she admitted. "You do business from this place?"

"Theoretically," he said with a sigh, and stopped to lock the door behind them. "Not in a very long time."

Snatching up a frayed cardboard box from the corner, he swept the contents of the desktop into it and made his way around the room adding papers and bottles he picked up from the floor.

"I didn't remember quite how bad it was," he told her. "But it seemed like a safer place to hide than the boat."

"It's fine," she told him in a conciliatory tone. "Beggars can't be choosers."

"It's just for one night."

"It's fine," she repeated, hoping that he believed her.

"Sit down," he told her, tucking the box under his arm as he lifted the brimming trashcan and headed for the door.

"There might be a Coke in the fridge. I'll be back in two shakes."

Raine surveyed her surroundings with a grimace once he'd gone. The place was nothing less than a pigsty!

Stepping over a pile of manila files, she slid the wig from her head and tossed it to the desktop as she made her way to the far wall to examine the cluster of framed photographs. Most of them depicted a much younger, more cleancut Ray in his police uniform with various officials and fellow officers. One of them drew her curious attention, and Ray stepped up behind her just as she approached for a closer look.

"That was my father."

"He was a police officer too?"

"Yes, for the Cleveland department. That was taken just a few weeks before his death."

"Did he die while on duty?" she asked cautiously.

"He was murdered after testifying in the case of a local criminal with mob connections," he told her, then crossed over to the small square refrigerator on the floor by the window and produced a beer. "There's Coke, if you want one."

"No, thank you. Maybe later," she replied without taking her eyes off the man in the photograph. He looked like a young Elvis Presley, dressed up like a cop for a movie role. "You look a lot like your father. You definitely have his eyes."

"A lot of people say that."

Raine turned back to find Ray lounged out on half of the long brown couch, tipping back a bottle of beer.

"Is he the reason you became a cop yourself?" she asked, then gingerly lowered herself to the sofa beside him.

"I guess so," he replied somberly. "And maybe the reason I want to nail Carmichael so badly. They never pinned my parents' murder on the guy who ordered it from the inside."

"Your mother too?" she asked, her heart pounding out a sympathetic rhythm.

"I was spending the weekend fishing with the family of one of my buddies."

"Were they . . . at the house? The one in Walt Whitman?"

Ray nodded, then took several swallows of beer before adding, "I guess I just want to see someone like him get what's coming."

"And all the while I thought I was the reason you wanted to get Harrison."

"You were the reason that came later," he said, running two fingers down the length of her arm from her shoulder.

"Ray, will you tell me something, please?"

"If I can."

"What's the thing they offered you? The reason you let yourself be recruited by the FBI in the first place?"

Ray sighed, then took one more long draw from the beer bottle before placing it on the floor next to his foot.

"Exoneration," he stated simply.

"From?"

"I was a cop for fourteen years. In homicide for six. I was investigating the murder of a prostitute down on the wharf, a young girl nobody gave a damn about. Just your typical homicide."

"Until?"

"Until things started adding up. A link to a councilman. And the next thing I knew, I was brought up on charges for accepting bribes in return for favors."

"Bribes?" she said with a hint of a chuckle. "You wouldn't take a bribe."

"How do you know that?" he asked seriously. "I mean . . . How can you be so sure?"

She was almost afraid to ask. "Did you?"

"No. I didn't."

"I knew you wouldn't," she stated simply.

"Well, you and nobody else. The charges were completely bogus, but I could never prove it. I lost my job and my pension, my reputation. There was no turning back."

"So you moved to a houseboat in La Jolla."

"Got a license to investigate," he finished for her. "And built . . . all this."

She looked around at the meager surroundings and smiled sadly.

"My heart wasn't in it," he said on a groan. "I guess I kind of let it go to crap."

"And they promised you exoneration?"

"Cort came to me and said if I'd go undercover, find out what you knew about Carmichael, why you left in such a hurry, kept you out of harm's way until they could find out what you might have to offer, they would pave a way to vindicate me."

"So if this turns out the way they want, you'll go back to being a cop?"

"Nah." He sighed. "But my name will be cleared, and I'll get my benefits back."

"That's very important to you, isn't it? For your name to be cleared."

"As a cop, that's all there is. Your reputation."

"So," Raine supposed, "let's say it all works out. Harrison is in jail, you've done your part, and your name is cleared. What then?"

Ray thought that through for several long moments, then let a wistful smile wind around his entire face. "I don't know. Maybe I'll start a little bed and breakfast."

Raine's heart fluttered at the thought, and she slid across the couch into Ray's arms just as he opened them to her.

* * *

"Why can't you just bring him in? You've got a witness to Joe Dunne's murder. Isn't that enough?"

Raine rose up on her elbow and looked at Ray leaning over his desk, the telephone to his ear. From the look of him, she doubted that he'd gotten any sleep at all.

She jumped as Ray pounded his fist hard against the desktop. "What do you mean? Where's our witness, Cort?"

A wave of nausea rose from the pit of her stomach.

"Just another reason to do things my way Cort. I'll be in touch."

"Another setback," she surmised as Ray folded the cellular and set it down on the table beside the couch.

"For the moment," he replied, but she knew his optimism was forced for her benefit alone. "You look like you could use some time in the sun. What do you think of some time out on the water?"

"What did you have in mind?" she asked, trying to sound upbeat. "A day spent sailing out on the Pacific?"

"Something like that. Not for a joy ride, though." He lowered himself next to her and suddenly looked very serious. "I thought we could sail down to Mexico. We could stick close to Rosarito and Puerto Nuevo. It's not far enough from the border to be troublesome, but far enough that you'll be safe for a while."

"And then what?" she asked him. "Do I just keep running for the rest of my life?"

"No," he replied in raspy emotion. "The department is working to nail Carmichael. Once that happens and he's put away, you'll be free to go wherever you want to go. Until then, I'm afraid—"

"I'm a prisoner," she finished for him, tears forming in her eyes.

"Is that what you feel like when you're with me? A prisoner?"

"No, Ray," she said, moving toward him and leaning into

his chest. "You're the only good thing about this whole ordeal."

She wrapped her arms around him and moved her fingers slowly up his back, nestling her cheek into his chest. It was a moment before he reciprocated in any way, but finally he held her there.

"What if I went back?" she suggested carefully.

"Back where?"

"Back to Harrison."

Ray pulled her away from him and looked hard into her eyes. A whole range of emotions moved across his face in only an instant. Hurt. Rage. Anger. Betrayal.

"You want to go back to him?"

"No, of course not," she explained. "But I could try and work my way back into his trust. I could find things. Gather information." She had the desperate feeling of someone who was making it up as she went along. In part, it sounded as absurd to her as it obviously did to Ray. And in another part, somewhere deep down inside of her, she clung to the belief that it could work. That she could speed up the whole process.

"You could get yourself killed!" he snapped. "Are you out of your mind?"

"He loves me," she tried hard not to shout. "Or at least he's obsessed with me. He'll take me back and he'll believe me. I'll make him believe me!"

"If he loves you so much, why did he beat you and lock you away like an animal? I am not willing to take any stupid chances with your life, Raine."

"He thinks I've turned against him," she said assuredly. "But I could convince him otherwise. I know I could."

"Forget it," he said certainly. "It's a crazy idea. We'll do it my way."

Pushing her away from him, Ray got up and stalked out

of the office. A moment later, she heard the men's room door slam down the hall.

It wasn't such an outlandish plan, she groaned to herself. It was dangerous, yes, but it was just as dangerous to keep running. Every night in a different place. Every day hoping not to be discovered, afraid to walk around the corner or look up into the face of a stranger. She couldn't keep living this way, and she had to convince Ray somehow that they had to take some action.

He was the most stubborn man she'd ever met!

Ray was gone for a long while, leaving Raine alone in the huge, empty room. It was like a cavern. Silent and cold, the distance between them stretched out like a field of dry grass, not even a breeze to break up the stillness.

She didn't know how long she had been sitting there, motionless on the edge of the couch, frozen like a doll. It seemed like an eternity before she finally heard him close the door down the hall. When he came back in, he did so in silence, lowering down into the squeak of the office chair without so much as a word to her.

Oh, he was quite the man in charge, she thought. Smooth as glass until he didn't get exactly what he wanted. Until he was no longer in complete and utter control. And then he turned on her with the indifference of a stranger.

Raine smacked both hands down hard against her sides and an involuntary groan escaped from deep inside her throat. His silence angered her, and at the same time it cut through her like a sharp, shiny knife wielded carelessly in the dark. She'd made one simple suggestion. Okay, so he didn't like it—even wouldn't allow it—but why must he punish her for the very thought of it? And that was what Ray's silences did to her, they punished her. She unconsciously compared them to the beatings that Harrison delivered, and then felt ashamed of herself for the contrast.

Raine pulled clean clothes slowly from the suitcase propped open on the chair against the wall. She folded a few items across her arm and picked up the small zippered case of toiletries, and then left the office in the same still silence he had created.

In the bathroom down the hall, she scrubbed her face and brushed her teeth, squinting to catch her image in the dreary, cracked mirror on the wall before her. She could almost see him there in the reflection, tucked away in his silent office, his black hair mussed, falling in inadvertent wisps across those beautiful eyes which were encircled by deep, dark lashes that rested in thick tufts upon his tan skin.

Raine felt her inner demeanor begin to soften at the thought of him like that, and her anger drifted from her like so many puffs of vapor. Her affection for Harrison had been a wordless, dignified sort of love initially, born out of girlish regard for his command of life, for his power and presence. What was developing toward Ray, however, was more like a raging fire spreading out over a hillside. Everything about him aroused her, and she found that she spent more and more of her quiet time—what little there was of it of late—struggling against her own feelings.

And when she finally let it, the word *love* had dropped on her like a stone down the shaft of a well, and she'd been walking around with the bruise from it ever since.

Chapter Nine

Raine took her time getting cleaned up and dressed. She wanted to give Ray as much time alone as she could, hoping that her return would find him in better spirits.

"I'm so hungry," she announced as she walked back into the office half an hour later. "What about you?"

Her words trailed off and her tennis shoes squeaked to a halt atop the cracked tile of the floor as she found herself face-to-face with a stranger.

"Ray!" she called as she began to back up, but the stranger lifted his hand toward her with a smile that tried to tell her everything was all right and that he belonged there.

"I'm Ben Travis," he assured her. "I'm a friend of Ray's."

"Ray?" She couldn't take her eyes off him, and her frozen feet fastened her to that spot.

"You met my wife? Sage?"

Ben had light sandy hair, and his eyes were crystalline and kind.

"Oh!" Ray exclaimed, and he wrapped his arm around

Raine's shoulder as he stepped up beside her. "It's all right, Raine. This is Ben. He's giving us a ride to the marina."

"Sorry," Raine apologized as she took his outstretched hand. "Ray is teaching me to be so cautious that it borders on rude sometimes."

"I understand." He grinned. "Better to be safe than sorry."

"There's coffee and muffins on the desk," Ray pointed out. "Go ahead. We'll be heading out in a few minutes."

"Heading out where?"

It wasn't long before she had the answer to that question and Ben cheerfully waved good-bye to them as Ray expertly guided a large yacht named *The Tequila Sunrise* away from the dock they'd driven out to and set sail into more choppy sea waters.

"We're going to Mexico?" she asked him, but Ray only nodded. "Is this your boat?"

Again, he nodded. But she had the feeling that he wasn't planning to answer anything until they were well on their way.

The Pacific Ocean was as blue as a sparkling sapphire under the morning sun, and Raine shed the denim overshirt she donned over a white tank T-shirt, which was tucked loosely into a pair of dark denim jeans. She could feel Ray's eyes upon her as she stretched out on the deck under the sun, but she didn't let on that she did.

"Any sunscreen aboard?" she called out without turning around.

"No," he replied strangely. Then after a moment, she looked back to find him kneeling beneath the steering column, fiddling intently with something she couldn't manage to see.

"What are you doing?" she asked, but he didn't answer. "Ray?"

Several moments passed before he rose up again, his face

washed pale, and Raine cocked her head slightly as their eyes met.

"What is it?"

"Come here," he finally said softly.

Something in his voice caused her to hesitate, and she repeated, "What is it, Ray?"

"Come here."

Raine quickly pulled herself to her feet and tied the denim shirt in a knot around her waist as she approached. When she reached him, Ray nodded in the direction of the floor of the steering column.

Raine gasped when she saw it. The panel was pulled back to expose several wires twisted around a red canal with what looked like the face of a clock attached.

"Ray?"

"It was set to go off within an hour of the engine turning over," he told her. "Someone figured out where we were headed before I did."

"We're not staying on this boat!" she exclaimed. "Turn this thing around right now, Ray! . . . Or I know! Let's jump ship! Come on."

Raine hurried to the side of the boat and tossed one leg over, then looked back and nodded to Ray. "Let's go!"

Ray held the wheel with one hand and reached out for her with the other. "It's disconnected now," he said as he invited her back. "For the moment, anyway. Hear me out?"

Raine cautiously climbed down and inched toward him, tears standing in her wide eyes. "I hate this," she told him as she fell into his embrace. "I hate this whole thing."

"I know you do," he seemed to be almost chuckling. "I know, honey."

"Who did this?" she finally asked him. "How did they know we would go out on your boat?"

"From the looks of things, I think they must have rigged

it once they found out we were in San Diego. Just a hunch perhaps."

"What are we going to do now? Do you have a plan?"

Ray grinned at the uncertainty with which she had asked him that question. "Yes."

"What is it?"

"Can you swim?"

"Yes. Very well."

"Good."

They hadn't come across more than five other vessels since they'd crossed the border into Mexican waters, and Puerto Nuevo was a mere three or four miles down the coast. Ray was relieved that there would be no traffic on the water when the thing blew; he couldn't have some innocent bystanders out for a pleasure trip getting hurt.

He glanced at Raine, stretched out on her stomach at the tip of the bow like a cat settled on a window sill. She looked completely at ease, no hint of the knowledge that a bomb was aboard, that they were going to have to set it off, jump ship and hope that they swam fast enough not to be injured in the debris when it blew.

He remembered the look in her eye when she'd held Coleman's gun on the man, a look of determination, almost desperation. The look of someone who would do whatever they had to do. And he loved that about Raine. Even at her most vulnerable, she was always able to snatch herself up by the bootstraps, find some strength from somewhere deep inside her and do whatever she had to do at the moment.

The huge sun flamed like a monstrous daffodil in the sky, its petals of yellow fire reaching in every direction, and it touched down on Raine's back as soft and silky as a purring kitten.

Just then, she turned over and sleepily faced him. "Are we almost there?"

"You'd better start waking up," he replied.

In the distance, several sailboats moved gently across the water like large, white butterflies that had dipped down to take a drink, and there was no other activity in any direction.

"You ready?" he asked her as she moved toward him.

"No."

Well, at least she was no liar.

"That is Puerto Nuevo," he pointed out. "Right where the tip of the land juts out. And that stretch of white beach just beyond it is where we're going to try and come out."

Raine nodded thoughtfully, and Ray admired her calm.

"I've been watching the current," he continued. "We'll go just a bit further."

"Okay."

There were no more than five people on the beach where he was planning their arrival, and he knew the natives of that particular area to keep pretty much to themselves. Even if the Federalis became involved, no one would be knocking down their door to serve as witnesses. He and Raine would just come up on the beach like happy swimmers, he went over in his mind. Assuming that took them fifteen minutes, they would be up on the beach by the time the ship blew.

The Tequila Sunrise was like a longtime friend, and it saddened Ray to lose her. But if all went well, it would be worth ten vessels just like her. No, a hundred. Keeping Raine safe was all that mattered to him any more.

He hadn't noticed her approaching, but the warmth of her skin against his drew his attention immediately. Raine leaned over him with a weary smile and ran a finger along his forehead.

"Are those worry lines about me?" she asked, and he knew that she could read his mind.

"Yes."

"Well, put them away. I have complete faith that we're going to pull this off. I have complete faith . . . in you."

She never ceased to amaze him.

Raine bent down toward him and touched his lips lightly with hers. He couldn't seem to help himself, and Ray wrapped his arms tightly around her waist and pulled her down to his lap. When they finally parted, he noticed that her beautiful red lips were slightly swollen from the pressure of him, and her sleepy eyes reflected his own desire.

Raine moved in toward him and kissed him again, this time sweetly, like the gentle melody of a song he knew by heart. He straightened his long legs and slowly stood, sliding Raine from him to a standing position as well.

"Put your shirt on," he told her as he wrapped a change of clothes in a plastic waterproof sack and sealed it tight. "That water can get awfully cold."

When he was through, Ray pulled the metal panel away from the makeshift bomb.

"You go on and get a head start," he urged, but Raine didn't budge.

"No," she seemed to plead. "I want us to go in together."

He resisted the urge to fight her on it and just shot her a quick smile before setting to work on the wires. With one more snap and a short twist it was done.

"Okay," he said. "Let's roll."

Each of them tossed a leg over the side, and then another. One last look at each other, eyes locked, and they jumped into the chilly water and began the long swim toward the shore.

The undertow was a bit stronger than Ray had anticipated, and he knew if he was having trouble negotiating it, Raine might find herself in trouble. He stopped, breathless, searching the waters around him for her form, and he found it just a few yards behind him.

"You okay?" he called, and she answered with a nod and a slight groan.

Fatigue swept over Raine in flurries at first, then like a tropical storm. Her arms ached as she pressed them out and pulled them back, moving herself along in the cold sea. The road ahead seemed unending, and she could no longer see Ray in front of her. Just the deep blueness of the sea and the distant promise of land.

"Ray," she tried to call, but his name was drowned inside her mouth as it filled with thick, salty water.

She couldn't make it any further. The pull of the water beneath her was strong and unwavering. She tried to remember the taste of Ray's kiss and then bribe herself with the promise of another once she made it to land, but the memory washed from her as she was pulled under yet again.

On the third time, the sea formed an icy hand with long, pointed fingers that wrapped around her ankle and yanked her down beneath the surface of the water. Panic broke from her and simple weariness was her anchor, like a crushing weight upon her as she plummeted downward.

The rush of water tore through her eardrums, and she closed her eyes so tightly that she began to see bursts of stars.

My life is over.

And pictures, like quick reels of film, steamrolled across her mind.

Pain suddenly rang an alarm straight through her, and she felt herself twist beneath it like laundry in a harsh wind. It wasn't until she came back to the surface, spitting and sputtering for air, that she realized Ray had pulled her up by the first thing he could grab. Her hair.

"Ray!" she squealed gratefully when she saw him, and

she threw her arms around his neck and pulled them both under the water again.

"Whoa!! Whoa," he shouted, and he slipped his arm around her waist. "W-work with me here," he stammered as he began to swim away, Raine in tow.

Suddenly, a thunderous explosion vibrated the sea around them, and waves crashed up over them and took them under once again. When they came to the surface, Ray propped Raine to her feet, and she dug her toes into the glorious sand beneath her.

Behind them, fire rose beneath black columns of smoke from the water, and debris from their boat seemed to litter every direction. People on the shore rushed into the water, knee-deep, in order to get a closer look. The last thing they were aware of was the American couple emerging from the water and standing beside them in the sand.

After a few moments, Ray gently pulled Raine away from the shore. He held tightly to her hand, released it when one of the donkeys in the stopgap stable on the sand came between them, and then they clasped hands once again. Raine's legs felt as if they were rubber and she thought she might collapse except for the support of Ray beside her, his free arm around her waist, partially carrying her.

They checked into the hotel as Mr. and Mrs. David Sommer.

"We'll hit the sack early," Ray told her as he shut the door behind them. "Tomorrow, we'll start across Mexico and enter back through Texas."

Raine couldn't stop herself, and she burst into tears, sobbing into her hands like a little child.

"What is it?" he asked as he took her into his arms. "You need a warm bath, some grub and a good night's sleep, sweetheart. You're going to be fine."

"I almost drowned," she sputtered back at him. "I was only a moment away from dying, Ray. And you pulled me out. You saved my life."

After a long moment, he grinned at her and asked, "Are you thanking me?"

"Y-yes," she stammered with a lopsided smile. "Thank you."

Ray brushed her mouth with a tender kiss.

"You know what I was thinking about when I went under?"

"No. What?"

"I was thinking about you, and what it feels like to kiss you. What your skin feels like when I touch it. What the future holds for us, if anything. I thought I was going to die right then, and I was grieving for all the things we never had together."

Ray guided her head to his shoulder, and then smoothed her hair down against his chest.

"You know that I'm falling in love with you, don't you?" she asked softly, but she didn't look up to face his silence.

"No," he said finally. "I didn't."

Raine's eyes widened, and she looked at him squarely, her irises deepening in color.

"You didn't?"

Ray didn't answer. After a moment, he ran a hand through his straight black hair and brushed it away from his face.

"Raine," he began, and then looked away. "I—"

"Thank you," she blurted. "Thank you very much."

He looked stunned as she flew from the bed and into the bathroom.

"You couldn't have stopped me?" she cried from the doorway. "You couldn't see that coming and stop me from humiliating myself?"

"Raine, listen to me . . ."

"I've listened to you too much already," she accused,

then stalked back across the room and stood in front of him. With a raised finger to his face, she brought herself into full control. "You . . . kissed me . . . and held me . . . and allowed me to believe that feelings were growing in you too. What was that, Ray? Just another way of yours to keep me in line? Well, let me tell you something, Martin. I can read you like a book now. Keep your hands to yourself, and your lips too. Let's just do this thing, whatever it is, and get it over with. After that . . ."

"Raine."

"After that," she repeated, smoldering, "don't ever come near me again."

That said, she turned on her heels and stomped back to the bathroom and slammed the door. Leaning against it, the tears came in waves, rolling down her face in streams, begging for sobs to accompany them, but Raine wasn't going to give him the satisfaction.

Suddenly, the bathroom door burst open and she was thrust away from it and into the counter. It took her a moment to catch her breath, but when she did, she was already being dragged out by her arm and nudged over to the bed.

"Oh, I get it," she seethed up at him. "Now that it's all out in the open, you show your true colors."

"Would you shut up long enough to listen to me?" he raged, and then smacked his fist against the mattress beside her. "Just . . . shut . . . up!"

Raine couldn't help herself, and she spat at him, right in the face.

Ray's eyes misted over with angry emotion. He wiped the insult away, then looked down at her coldly.

"If you're through . . . you're going to listen to me, and you're not going to say another word until I tell you what I have to say."

"Fine."

"That's another word," he said in a threatening voice. "Now . . . be . . . quiet."

"Fine."

He shook his head and puffed out a sigh of frustration. "I wanted to tell you that I have feelings for you too."

"Oh, really." Her voice was as cold as stone.

As she looked up into those dark brown eyes of his, she felt as if he were an inferno, melting her suddenly and without effort.

She could hardly believe it, but several large, salty tears fell down his face like raindrops on a window. He was crying!

"Ray?"

The whites of his eyes burned red, and he sniffed back the emotion that had seeped out before he crossed the room. His hand on the knob, he looked back at her, still lying on the bed where he'd left her, a crumpled paper after a violent storm.

"I love you too," he half-whispered, then walked out the door.

It was a very long time before Raine could pull herself up and, when she did, she sat there frozen on the edge of the bed. Had she heard him correctly?

I love you, too.

The words tore at her heart, leaving painful, searing burns inside her chest. If he loved her, why did he turn to stone when she had declared the same feelings for him? Just like the night before at his office. She made a simple suggestion that he didn't agree with, and his response had cut her like a knife.

This was not going to be an easy man to love.

In her head, Raine knew that Ray would be back. As volatile as he could be where some things were concerned, she knew he was not the kind of man who would leave her in a strange hotel in a foreign country. He was the kind of man, she supposed, who was driven to "finish" things, and her situation was far from being finished.

The closest thing to elegant she could find in the lobby gift shop was a white floral tank dress. It was made of cotton T-shirt material and she liked the way the torso of the dress laced up the back, and how the skirt billowed to tea-length just a couple of inches above the ankle.

After a hot shower, she climbed into the dress and placed a bit of foundation and blush on her sun-reddened face. Room service sent up a lovely array of fruits and sweets along with two sandwiches on fresh croissant rolls. She had ordered a pitcher of chilled raspberry juice and two crystal wine glasses along with an assortment of candles that they managed to assemble at her request, and she moved the table closer to the window to overlook the view of the ocean at sunset.

The front desk helped her out by promising to send up as many roses as they could spare from the lobby arrangement, which happened to be six, and she used them to produce fragrant petals that she spread over the table and the floor around it. And just when she began having thoughts of the dozen candles scattered about the room burning down to nothing before he ever returned, Ray came quietly through the door.

"Hungry?" she asked him sweetly from the table by the window.

Ray took a long moment and looked around at the elaborate care she had taken to prepare for his return and a smile curled quickly across his face. He looked boyish just then, like a child who'd received his first Valentine. Raine loved the way that smile washed over him, a smile that took with it his whole face, his eyes, and his emotions.

Raine rose gracefully from the chair and stepped toward him, her hand outstretched. He took it in a way that got to her, in a shy way, as if he were unsure of where they were going. She led him to the table and released his hand, then sat down and motioned for him to do the same.

"You didn't answer me," she said as she removed the silver domed covers from their food. "Are you hungry?"

"Very."

"Well," she said and grinned from ear to ear, "dig in."

Ray took a large bite from the sandwich as she filled his glass with deep red juice. She tried not to watch him, but she had a hard time taking her eyes from him. His skin was washed with color, a tell-tale sign that he'd been out in the sun most of the time that he'd been gone, and his dark eyes were lined in amber strain. The black silken hair that always rebelliously refused to stay out of his face had fallen forward, unruly and mussed.

When he had taken the last bite of his sandwich, Ray stole two strawberries from the sterling bowl and popped them into his mouth. Then, tossing the linen napkin from his lap to the table, he leaned back, propping his right ankle casually upon his left knee, and regarded her with an intense smile.

"What?"

"This is quite a little scene you have going here." He grinned. "What's the occasion?"

"Well, it's not every day," she replied, trying to disguise the uneasiness poking her in the stomach like a large, jagged rock, "that the man I love tells me . . . he loves me too."

"Oh," he replied, and then looked out the window for a long moment.

"Do you want to tell me what that was all about before?"

He glanced back at her, seriousness rising over him like steam. "I'm a great marksman, did you know that?"

"No," she chuckled. "Is that right?"

"I hold a black belt in martial arts, and I've been honored

twice by the department for going above and beyond the call of duty."

"That's . . . very interesting."

"At one time I single-handedly brought two rival gangs to their knees by smoking their kingpin out of hiding and into the hands of the authorities. But you . . ." He looked at her so hard that it tickled. "You are a whole other story."

"Are you saying you'd rather be here right now with someone from a gang?"

"It would be easier for me to bear my soul to him, yes." They shared a laugh over that, but Ray turned hotly serious again. "Love is a very difficult emotion for me to come to terms with," he told her as he traced circles in the crumbs left behind on the table near his plate.

"I could help you," she offered with a sincere smile. "If you'd let me."

"Your life is at risk," he said, his voice level raising an octave or two. "And I am responsible for seeing to it that you make it out of this ordeal alive. How can I do that effectively when I have to fight these bouts of drowning in my feelings for you?"

"You don't have to drown," Raine told him as she rose to her feet and approached him. She daintily stooped before him and placed both hands on his crossed leg. "Neither of us do. We can be life preservers for each other instead."

Ray unfolded his leg and pulled Raine to his lap, wrapping her into his arms and nuzzling his face into her perfumed hair, the only light in the room now burning from the candles and filtering in through the window.

"After everything you've been through," he whispered, eyes closed and face buried, "after all he did to you . . . How can you still believe in love so completely?"

"I didn't think I could," she told him, pulling back to look him squarely in the eye. "Until now."

Chapter Ten

Dawn brought with it sunlight which dropped through the window in a shower of golden beams. Ray propped himself up on one elbow and looked over at the other bed. He spent a good bit of time simply watching the rise and fall of Raine's breathing. She was a vision.

How could it be that someone so perfectly beautiful and tender could fall for the likes of me?

For a moment, he toyed with the notion that he'd been dreaming and the previous night would fray away from him at any moment like the threadbare knees of his favorite pair of jeans, but when Raine opened her eyes and grinned up at him as if he were the only man on the face of God's earth, his heart pounded gratefully at the reality. They were in love, he and she. This flawless culmination of everything he wanted out of life had actually found it within her to love him. And he loved her with every breath left inside him.

"Morning," she whispered.

"You know, I've been thinking," he returned, stretching out his arm, then leaning back upon the elbow. "You will marry me when this is over, won't you?"

"Marry you?"

"Yes. Will you?"

"Of course." She grinned, and her smile was to him like all of the miracles of a bright Christmas morning.

"Good." He shot her a wink before continuing on without missing a beat. "Then I think we have to do something to speed up this process. I want to marry you before Christmas. Any problem with that?"

"I'll check my calendar."

"I've been giving a lot of thought to that idea of yours," he said, climbing from bed and snatching up the phone. "Two western omelettes and a pot of herbal tea with two cups," he told room service. "Yes, thank you."

"What idea of mine have you been giving thought to?" she asked excitedly, sitting upright and pulling the blankets around her.

"The one about going back."

The green of Raine's eyes turned almost black as she stared at him. "Are you serious?"

"Were you?"

"Yes, if you think we can pull it off."

"It could be very dangerous, Raine." Concern filtered from his eyes across her entire body. "And we'll take no stupid chances. You won't try to have contact with him at all."

"I have a few thoughts about that," she suggested hopefully, but she could see that he wanted to shut her off if only he could find the switch. "Listen to me, Ray. It could work."

"Not if it involves your trying to get back into his good graces. He's smarter than you give him credit for, Raine."

"My idea doesn't involve that kind of risk. All we'll need is an invitation to a party."

Ray looked at her curiously, and Raine smiled from ear to ear, beaming with enthusiasm to share her revelation.

She'd remembered in the middle of the night. It had dropped upon her like a sudden bolt of lightning, and she had been relieved when Ray brought up the subject out of the blue. One well-placed call, and they were in business!

"Hello?" Ray crooned into the receiver in his best English accent. "Yes, I'd like to speak to someone about the annual fundraiser ball . . . Yes, I attended a couple of years back. It was held at the home of Mr. and Mrs. Harrison Carmichael . . . Correct. Will they be giving the usual soiree this year? . . . Excellent! When will the event be held? I'm afraid I haven't received my invitation. The pesky postal system, you know."

Raine covered her mouth to suppress the chuckle that rose in her throat, and Ray warned her to behave with the wiggle of one finger.

"Two weeks? Oh, dear. I'm afraid I'll be on the continent at that time. Drat. Well, perhaps next year. Thank you, dear."

When he hung up the phone, Raine shouted in amazement and tossed her arms around his neck, planting kisses along the side of his face. "You were fabulous!" she declared.

"Saturday, the twenty-third," he told her. "We have less than two weeks to put it all together."

"We can do it!" she assured him. "We can!"

The trip through Mexico was relatively uneventful except for the very difficult time they had finding a decent bathroom. The moment they crossed the border into Texas, they stopped for refueling, both the car and themselves.

"A hamburger with the works and a vanilla shake," Raine cooed at Ray. "I'm going to clean up a little."

Mexican highways were dusty and remote, and it was a

relief just to be back in the land of burgers, bathrooms and vending machines. She deposited all the change she could find in the bottom of her purse in the slot and, in return, it dropped a candy bar and two packs of peanut butter crackers out of its large mouth, and Raine stuffed them into her purse for later.

In the bathroom, she splashed cool water on her face and washed with a damp paper towel, then smoothed lotion on her arms and hands from the travel pack she carried with her in the oversized leather satchel she'd bought at the hotel gift shop. She ran a quick brush through her hair and gathered it up in one hand, twisting it, then tying it into a knot at the top of her head. She wasn't sure it was going to stay there, but it did, just a few disobedient wisps falling to her shoulders.

Raine smoothed the pastel skirt of its wrinkles, and she re-adjusted the short, sleeveless white sweater. Suntanned skin peeked out beneath it, just the tiniest trace of belly. After replacing the cinnamon color to her lips, she closed up her purse and made her way into the diner and joined Ray at the table.

Ray reached across the table and took Raine's hand into his, looking deep into her eyes.

"A burger and a vanilla shake," the waitress drawled in a thick Texas stroke. "And for the gentleman . . . a sub with oil and vinegar. Anything else?"

"Nothing now," Ray replied, releasing Raine's hand and studying the meal before them.

"I'm starving," she stated before diving into the burger full-force.

"It was a long day's ride," he added.

Raine took several bites of the hamburger, and then wiped the traces of it from her mouth with a paper napkin from a streaked dispenser on the table. "How long do you think it will take us to get to New York?"

"A few days. Four, if we take it easy."

"Are we going to stop for the night?"

"I'd like to get a few more miles behind us first," he told her between bites.

"Sounds good," she said, and he smiled at her approval.

When they'd finished their meal, Ray left $15 cash on the table, and he and Raine walked outside, hand in hand, into the late afternoon sun.

"Oh, Ray, look," she cried, pointing out a rickety shack across the road sporting signs bearing the names of half a dozen fruits and vegetables. "Let's get something fresh for the road! I'd kill for a peach right now. Do you suppose they have peaches?"

She was a bit ahead of him and seemed to drag him along at a full trot as they crossed the road and headed across the small gravel parking lot toward the empty stand.

Raine popped a purple grape into her mouth and grinned at Ray. "Do you like seedless?"

Ray nodded, then picked up a pint of ripe strawberries and a cellophane pack of fresh red licorice. As they stepped up to the cash register where an elderly woman stood waiting, Raine grabbed a package of cashews from the metal rack and added it to their pile of purchases.

"Munchies." She grinned at the woman, already tugging open the nut bag and digging in.

"That'll be nine-sixteen," she returned with a toothy grin, and Ray slipped her a $10 bill as the woman placed the fruit into a plastic bag.

Raine hurried back into the diner when they crossed the street and into the bathroom to wash the grapes and berries while Ray brought the car to the door and waited for her. Something about the way he looked at her as she stepped back out of the diner caused her heart to leap slightly from its place, and then fall back again as it pounded wildly.

When she climbed into the car, she leaned over and planted a warm kiss on his stubbly cheek.

"What was that for?" he asked curiously.

"No reason," she said with a lazy sigh.

She felt safe, and, what was more, she was enjoying the road trip with Ray. They were quietly comfortable with each other, amiable travel companions, like two spoons that fit nicely together in the drawer. Sometimes they chatted about the scenery or the weather, other times they just held hands while Raine sang softly with the radio. Whatever was going to happen in New York, Raine knew she would never forget this time with Ray. It was her gift, and she happily intended to make the most of every moment.

Chapter Eleven

Three glorious days on the road together had passed, and when they crossed the border into the State of New York, neither one of them felt fully prepared for whatever stretched out ahead of them. They'd gone over and over it as they approached their destination, so many times that Raine was almost sick of hearing her own voice.

They would check into the Sumner Inn and get cleaned up, then Ray would walk through town to the old Village Printers building on the corner of Main and Alliance. The New York Endowment for the Arts fundraiser ball held every year at the compound was by invitation only, and the invitations were always printed up by Manny, then addressed and mailed by June Devonshire, the local calligrapher with her own rented desk in the corner of the print shop. If memory served, the invitations would be within a day or two of being mailed out, and she and Ray would have arrived in town just in time. They had to get their hands on two invitations.

Raine had been planning this particular gala for years on end, and she could supply him with the details, but Ray would have to be the one to enter Village Printers and inconspicuously make off with the parchment cards.

If anyone could do it, Ray could. She told herself that again and again as she paced across the floor of their suite at the Sumner Inn. She had watched him out the window until she couldn't any more, until the last speck of him had disappeared around the corner of Main, until that final sway of narrow hips, and then the right turn up Alliance.

It had been only five minutes at the very most, but Raine felt as if he'd been gone for hours. Her palms were wet with perspiration, and her temples throbbed with impatient anticipation.

He's an ex-cop, for pete's sake. Surely, he can steal a couple of 3×5 cards from the desk of June Devonshire!

"May I help you?"

June smoothed the fire-engine orange hair that danced around her face in tousled curls with long, pointed fingers painted with a similar glossy shade.

"Yes, I hope so." Ray returned her smile and walked over to the edge of her desk. "I'd like to get some prices on printing a brochure."

"Oh, well, I'll have to get Manny for you," she suggested, but never budged to follow through.

Ray could feel the fabric of his shirt burn against his chest with the heat of her gaze. She had the look of someone who hadn't had lunch in three or four days. And he seemed to be the succulent feast spread out unwillingly before her.

"Who can I tell him is calling?" she purred at him.

"Trey Burroughs," Ray replied without missing a beat.

"And what line of business are you in, Mr. Burroughs? Or may I call you Trey?"

"Oh, Trey, please." He grinned. "And you are . . . ?"

"June Devonshire," she returned, and she seemed to follow her outstretched hand right across the desk with the dance of a rattlesnake in heat.

Ray took her hand and planted a tiny kiss at the base of the center knuckle, careful to avoid the spike of shiny fingernails that pressed into the skin of his palm.

"Oooh, how charming," she frothed like an endless chain of bubbles. "I'll tell Manny you're here. Don't go away now."

"My boots are nailed to the floor," he replied, the false smile dropping from his face the moment she disappeared, like lightning flashing from the sky.

He shuddered slightly before rounding the desk and flicking through the pile of envelopes she'd been working on when he arrived. Quickly, he opened one desk drawer, then another, finding nothing but files, miscellaneous office supplies and half a dozen shades of enamel nail polish.

Looking frantically around the room, Ray noticed several cardboard boxes in the corner, a 3×5" printed card taped to the lid of the one on the top. Hurrying to it, he scanned the script.

. . . cordially invited . . . annual masquerade ball . . . hosted by Harrison Carmichael . . .

Yes! This is it!

"Manny will be right with you, Mr. Burroughs," June drawled as she headed back into the room, and Ray snapped to attention so sharply that it pulled at the muscle in his neck. "I mean, Trey."

"Good!" he replied eagerly.

"He's on a telephone call in the back," she said as she smoothed her way against the entire width of him. "I guess I'll just have to keep you entertained until he's available."

"What a crying shame." He grinned from ear to ear, and then turned suddenly serious. "You know what would be truly helpful, Miss Devonshire?"

"June, please."

"June. Do you think you could round me up a price list?"

"Really, Manny is the one—"

"I'd consider it a personal favor," he interrupted, and June let out a long sigh of resignation before grinning at him.

"I'll see what I can do."

The moment she disappeared around the corner one more time, Ray sprang into action. In one smooth motion, he pulled one of the cards out of the box and replaced the lid. By the time she returned, he had slipped out the front door and made his way down the street and around the corner.

Minutes felt like hours, and hours like days. Ray had been gone such a very long time, and Raine's nerve endings were as raw as they possibly could be by the time he finally came through the door.

"Ray," she said as she rushed into his arms. "Did you get it?"

"One bright and shining invitation to a masquerade ball," he told her. "Now let's sit down and make our plans."

"One?" she questioned him, her eyes narrowed suspiciously.

"All we need is one."

"There are two of us."

"Oh, right. For me, and a guest."

"A guest? Really? I didn't remember that. Okay."

"All right. Now—"

"You wouldn't, would you?" she asked, and he looked at her curiously without reply.

"I wouldn't what?"

"Decide to leave me out of this."

"I couldn't if I tried, could I?"

Raine grinned at him and shook her head. "No."

"That's what I figured. Now let's get some paper and

sketch out a map of the place. Everything. The grounds, the entrance, and the way down to the secret room."

"Thank you, Ray."

"For what?"

"For keeping me in the loop," she told him. "Please don't decide to leave me out of this. Promise me."

"Raine, I told you—"

"Promise me."

"I promise."

She felt suddenly at ease with the uttering of those two little words. If there was one thing she could be sure about, it was that Raymond Martin was a man of his word.

Raine finally drifted off to sleep and dreamed about the bed and breakfast they would run in Walt Whitman, of seeing Grace again, of sipping tea out on the lawn, and of the tiny bookstore she had treasured so much where she'd first met Ray.

The dreamy vision of the old barn, the twinkling white lights, their first kiss in the snow that night . . . they crossed her mind's eye like previews at the movies. How she longed to go backward in time. Back to Ray's old house and that lovely barn. Back to the warmth and security of one of Grace's hugs. To hear the old woman call her "puppet," and to smell the fragrant honeysuckle that grew wild outside the back door.

"Raine?"

She jerked toward the sound of Ray's voice in the darkness, and tears gushed in streams down her face.

"You were calling out in your sleep," he told her from the doorway, and the concern in his voice lulled her in a way she'd never experienced before.

"Oh, Ray," she whimpered, and he moved toward her and engulfed her in his arms.

"What is it, darling?"

"Will we ever go back? Will things ever be right again?"

"They will," he assured her between kisses. "I promise you, they will."

Chapter Twelve

It warmed Raine inside to know the man so well. She looked at him just then over the rim of overflowing emotion. He was so beautiful. She traced his profile with her eyes, taking in every detail. The shine of his black hair, and the familiar stray lock that fell across his forehead and into his dark chocolate eyes. The cleft in his jaw, the determined lock of it as he made his endless notes.

There were pages and pages of them, yet he continued to scribble along. More to say, thoughts to add. He was going to go over it and over it until there was no margin for error, no matter how narrow. She adored that about him. The intensity of him. The sheer determination.

The sleeve of the denim work shirt he wore seemed to bulge with the muscular form of his biceps as the pen moved smoothly across the page. They were strong arms, and they were two more of the thousands of things she loved about Ray. Not overdone like the bodybuilder action heroes who might play Ray in a movie about their adventure. Just strong, developed and defined.

She closed her eyes for a moment and dreamed of the day that she could finally give herself to him, wholly and completely. When there would be no husband—no matter how much of a technicality Harrison was!—when they would be back in Walt Whitman, just the simple owners of a bed and breakfast, man and wife, members of the community.

The thought of it motivated her. She wished she could just will the day into full gear, that the evening would finally arrive so that they could get on with things. So they could resolve this mess and move on with the life she knew they would have together.

Mrs. Raymond Martin. It seemed to sing to her.

Raine Martin.

It was lyrical. And the name brought to mind a persona that seemed to match it. President of the PTA. Raine Martin. Mother of two . . . No, three. Her husband adores her and they live a quiet life up on the hill. Nothing special about them really. Except, of course, for the love they share.

"Did you hear me?"

"What?"

The voices of the future had been so loud that the present had been drowned out. Covered with sheets like old furniture.

"I'm sorry. What did you ask me?"

"Are you thinking of Walt Whitman?" He grinned.

"Yes," she admitted. "Walt Whitman a few weeks down the road when this is all behind us."

Ray fell quiet for a long moment, seemingly drifting forward to pick up where she'd left off if he could find it.

"What are you writing so frantically over there?" she asked as she rose from the sofa and made her way toward him.

"A jumbled mess," he chuckled, then tore the pages from the notebook and crumpled them between his two hands and tossed them effortlessly past her into the trashcan beneath the window. "Shall we start getting ready?"

"I'll go grab a shower," she replied, and then headed off toward the bathroom.

"Baby," he called to her softly, and she turned back to face him. "I love you."

Something in his eyes drew her back to him, and she fell into his arms as he kissed her long and deep and hard until her toes had begun to curl and her thoughts were about as far from Harrison and the mission they were on as she could ever have been.

When they were through, it took her a moment to bring back her senses. Her pulse was racing so fast that she could hear it in her ears, and her fingers tingled with the desire he had raised to the surface.

"Don't, Ray," she warned him.

"Don't what?"

"Don't kiss me like you're saying good-bye." Tears misted her eyes as she ran one hand through his silken hair. "We're going to get in and out of there tonight. And then it will be over."

Ray smiled at her, and it sent a shock wave through her entire body.

"I mean it," she insisted.

"I know," he replied.

"And I can do whatever I have to do."

He nodded. He seemed to know that, too.

"Everything's going to be okay."

"Yes. It will."

One last kiss and she moved into the bathroom and closed the door. It wasn't like Ray to be plagued with doubts like that. Tiny fibers tore inside her stomach. Something was eating him, and now it was eating her. What was it she had seen in those chocolate brown eyes of his?

She tried to put it behind her as she stepped into the

steaming hot shower. She could hear him moving around in the bedroom and she tried to fill her head with anything except the questions that ricocheted relentlessly from ear to ear. After a while she was able to do it too. Tune him out. Focus on nothing more than the rising steam and the pelting of water against her skin.

So much had happened since the last time she'd been inside the compound. She wondered how she would feel when faced with the prospect of reentering that world. She imagined herself walking up the three concrete steps—she still could remember that there were three!—to the massive front door and entering with all the other guests.

In years past, she had designed the floral arrangement for the round oak table at the center of the foyer and she casually wondered who had done it that year. Would Harrison have found anyone to take the painstaking time to sketch it out and meet with the florists in order to maintain the theme of the arts, or would he just have ordered a large vase of the most showy and elaborate stems? That part of the event was her favorite, the details and decorations, and Harrison had often chastised her for spending so much time on it.

"You're not designing a float for the Tournament of Roses here!" he had groaned the first year. "It's just flowers for the entry."

But to Raine it was a creative expression, the way all of her parties were an expression. It was one of the few things that ever made her valuable behind the walls of Harrison's compound and, no matter how he had complained about the time she invested in the projects, it was on the nights of those parties that she had felt most secure throughout her marriage.

She made him proud in the way she prepared the house and presented a table, in the way she draped herself on his arm as one more beautiful thing he could take credit for.

And making Harrison proud was the one way in which to tame him. Inflate the ego and the rest moved forcibly out of the way. It was the one safety valve she had been able to find once the first few months of their union had given way to the monster that lurked beneath Harrison's elegant facade.

The first explosion was more shocking than physically painful; it had consisted of nothing more than one hard slap across the face. So hard, in fact, that she'd fallen to the floor. It was followed up with six bouquets of lavender roses—her favorites—delivered at intervals throughout the day with cards bearing apologies and declarations of love still burning. The next incident didn't come for months but, when it did, it was followed up with more of the same. Lavender roses and empty promises. To that very day, Raine couldn't look at a lavender rose without the agonizing taste of bitterness and tears welling up at the back of her throat.

Entering the compound once again, this time on the arm of someone who truly loved and treasured her and valued her as more than a showpiece would be somewhat satisfying. Not that Harrison would even see them there together (at least, that's what she was praying for!), but there was some odd sense of vindication churning around inside her when she thought of returning there that night with Ray. The two of them together, working as a team to stamp out the final traces of that life with Harrison in order to raise a new life from the ashes.

When Raine stepped out of the shower that night, she felt cleansed, spiritually as well as physically. She was ready to face the mission ahead of them, and she could hardly wait to get on with it. Wrapped in a towel, she hurried out of the bathroom. Her arms ached with the need to embrace this man who had been instrumental in her deliverance.

"Ray?"

She had expected to see him sitting at the table where he'd been seated for days on end, and she was surprised when he wasn't. With a shrug, she padded barefoot across the thick carpet into the bedroom and stood at the center of the room and looked around.

"Ray?" she repeated, then sighed curiously.

For several moments, logical explanations ambled across her mind. Perhaps he'd run down to the gift shop for some toothpaste or a paper. Or out to the car to take a look at a map. Or had a sudden craving for a burger with everything. She tried hard to suppress the voice that kept whispering to her that he would have called out through the bathroom door to tell her where he was going had it been something so simple.

"Ray!" she called, this time more shrill and tainted with panic as she raced through the suite several times frantically. "Ray!!"

It wasn't until her third go-round that she noticed it there on the table and, as she approached it, she drew her breath in and held it there. A folded sheet of paper standing upright and facing her.

I'm sorry.
R.

"No!" she shrieked, then immediately pounded her fist against the tabletop so hard that the note fell over on its side. "You promised you wouldn't leave me out of it, Ray! You . . . *prom-ised.*"

Ray hated himself for breaking his word to Raine. But, he rationalized, he would have hated himself far more had she been caught in the crossfire while involved in something that was way over her head.

He imagined how angry and hurt she would be when she walked out of the bathroom to find that he was gone. Once it set in, she would run to the bedroom closet. He painted the scenario in transparent strokes on the windshield as he drove on. She would find the Tonto costume cut to shreds and lying in a heap on the floor behind the slatted oak door of the closet, his Lone Ranger duds nowhere to be found.

"It was the only way," he reasoned.

That costume was her ticket inside, and he was desperate to keep her out. Ray silently said a little prayer that she wouldn't do anything stupid. That she would wait there until he came back for her. And, most of all, that she would forgive him when he did.

He'd spent the better part of the afternoon trying to put it all on paper. How he loved her. How he would have died himself if anything would have happened to her. How desperately he wanted to protect her from Carmichael. He had glanced up at her a dozen times across the room as he scratched out his thoughts, struggling to make them congeal into something that made sense. And he'd finally tossed them into the garbage and settled for one simple statement.

"I'm sorry," he whispered.

And he was. But not sorry enough to go back for her. Not sorry enough to take her into the battle and take a chance on losing her. As far as Ray was concerned, Raine had done enough dying over Harrison Carmichael. He was going to step in on her behalf. If anyone was going to die that night, it wasn't going to be Raine.

Harrison Carmichael would never hurt her again. He vowed it, and Raymond Martin was a man of his word. At least, he always had been. Until that night.

Chapter Thirteen

Raine could hardly move from the spot. Nearly half an hour had passed, and she was still frozen there, that horrible note clenched in her hand, the terrycloth towel still wrapped around her.

"How could he?" she asked the air, and then squished another stream of tears out of her eyes before wiping them away with the back of her hand.

"I won't leave you out," she mocked, then slammed her fist hard on the tabletop once more. "I promise, he said."

Who did he think he was, she asked herself again and again. This was her future at stake, and she wanted a part in its outcome. He owed her that. After all, she'd provided all the information needed to move in. Ray had promised she wouldn't be left out.

Raine defiantly rose from the table and stomped into the bedroom.

"I won't be kept out!" she cried, tossing the closet door open so hard that it slammed against the wall behind it.

The sight of her shredded costume enraged her more than she would have thought possible. She gathered the tattered mess into her hands and fell to her knees just outside the closet. It was as if someone had used a blowtorch rather than a match to ignite her fury.

How could she ever have thought this man loved her? He didn't know her any better than this? He didn't sense how urgently important it was to her that he keep his word?

"I hate you!" she screamed, then threw the tattered costume to the floor and stalked from the room, seething.

"I . . . hate . . . you."

And she fully intended to hate Ray for the rest of her days over it, at least at first. She likened it to a *Reader's Digest* version of the stages of grief she had learned about in college as she moved from trying to blame herself for Ray's behavior to crying hysterically for long moments over the sheer betrayal of it. An hour passed before the fear finally set in, the worry for his safety. The panic.

Raine knew what kind of man Harrison was, and in that knowledge was an even fuller one. It was a distinct possibility that Ray would not come out of the evening alive. The one last thing Harrison could rob her of. The last joy he was able to take.

Raine wondered how long Ray had been plotting his betrayal. Had he known all afternoon? she asked herself. Had he known all along, or had he just decided in that one final instant? She remembered him sitting at the table, scratching his notes and making his plans. Plans she hadn't even been a part of, despite his promises to the contrary.

She glared harshly at the trash can where the crumpled paper still sat. Without forethought, she rose from her chair and approached it cautiously as if it might jump out at her. After a frozen instant of debate, she pulled the paper from the can and sat back down at the table, smoothing it out with her hand like an iron.

My darling . . .

They weren't notes at all. It was a letter. To her, presumably. Depending, of course, on how many other Darlings he was acquainted with!

My darling, she read again, then paused to draw in a deep, shaky breath before continuing.

I'm no poet, but something about you makes me wish I were. I'd like to write you sonnets and loves songs and whisper tender things to you that will keep you warm when you're lonely. But, as I say, I'm no poet.

No woman has ever brought out this side of me before, and I'm not quite sure what to do with this landslide of emotions you evoke every time we're close. Or even when we're not.

Like now. You're sitting on the couch across the room. Just sitting there! And I'm overwhelmed with love for you to the point of overflowing. I don't know how you do that from all the way across a room, but it's as if you were on this side of it, stroking me, just loving me.

A warm rush of solid heat made its way through Raine's veins just then, and she was forced to stop reading for a moment to clear her mind. If he truly loved her so much, why then did he betray her? Why did he make a promise he more than likely knew full well he never intended to keep?

A deep breath, and she could keep herself from the pages no longer.

By the time you're reading this, you will be standing on the edge of hatred for me because I've broken my word to you. And there's one thing that we have solid between us, and that's trust. It's been slow and steady in developing, but it's there and it tears me apart inside to betray that. I've tried and tried to talk myself out of it, to reason that I couldn't go ahead and leave you behind because I'd made that promise to you. But, Raine, darling, I can't justify it.

If I take you along tonight, in my heart I'm breaking a vow just as valuable. The one I made to myself when I fell in love with you. The one I've made to you nearly every day since this nightmare began for us. To take care of you. To protect you. To see you through to the happy ending.

We've grasped onto the picture of our future dream so tightly that it's become like a broken record we play again and again to assure ourselves that we'll make it through to the end. How can I waltz you into enemy camp tonight and risk your very life and lay all of that aside?

I thought about tying you to the chair, about locking you in this room while I ran off to resolve things. Anything to make sure you were safely tucked away until I could come back to you. The problem was . . . that made me into him. Harrison locked you away, and he robbed you of your dignity in doing so. Knowing, I couldn't turn around and do just that to you, too. All I can do is leave you behind, despite that promise I made not to, and hope that you'll understand that I did it out of love. That you will forgive me. That you'll wait here for me tonight for as long as it takes. That you'll be here when I get back.

Even as I'm writing, trying to explain, I still don't know if this is too much to ask. Or if I even have the right to . . .

The words that seemed to flow as smoothly as a river stopped there, suddenly and abruptly. Raine turned the last page over, searching for more, praying for more, but there was none.

She remembered the way he had tossed the pen to the table that afternoon as she approached him, how he had torn the pages loose and crumpled them in his hands. She had interrupted him. Or he had poured it out until he'd run dry. Either way, he had chosen to go another way. Rather than proclaim his deepest feelings and fears, he had chosen not to explain at all. A simple, "I'm sorry." As if that could say it all. As if that was the be-all and end-all of the story, the secret code that would cause Raine to bow down and wait for him like a good little girl until he came charging back on the white steed, the victor ready to explain his actions. Finally.

She couldn't help but wish he would have finished the letter. She noticed that her hands were trembling as she smoothed the pages out for the hundredth time, and she cursed the realization that had crept to the surface of her mind. Should something unforeseen happen that night, should Ray not emerge the victor and come charging back to her, she would have liked to have had this one letter to hold on to. Even unfinished, it would be what she would anchor herself to if she lost him.

She carefully straightened the corners of the one tangible remnant of his feelings for her. Something that, should he fail to return to her, would never let her forget that she had been loved, albeit too briefly, by Raymond Martin.

Ray's heart was pumping to maximum capacity as he filed slowly up toward the front door behind the crowd of party-goers. He hadn't expected such high security right at the get-go, and the way the two goons at the door gave "Rambo" and the plastic machine gun strapped to his chest the royal treatment, Ray was glad he'd decided to carry only the plastic variety of pistols with silver bullets in the holsters of his costume.

The two goons dissected him at the door like everyone else, then waved him on through without finding the Derringer he'd taped into the bowl of his Lone Ranger hat. It was small, but it was in and, if he found himself in a situation where he really needed it, he knew he wouldn't care about size in the least.

Ray nodded greetings to the reception line of representatives of the Endowment Fund, then moved carefully around the far side of the round oak table holding the monstrosity of plumes and foliage. Weaving through an endless stream of royalty and Einsteins and Abraham Lincolns, he made his way up several marble stairs to the open double doors of the library.

Ray snatched up a china plate and took a few moments' pause as he lingered over the prime rib to survey his surroundings. Everything was set up precisely as Raine had said it would be, right down to the smokers huddled in clumps outside on the patio. It wasn't hard for him to imagine her as the queen of this domain, and Ray found himself thinking that she pretty much belonged in a setting of elegance and grace.

He could imagine her floating from table to table, instructing caterers and placing the crystal in that just-so way she had about her. He smiled at the memory of the party she had orchestrated for his aunt's birthday, then chastised himself for not staying right on the ball. He'd been away from the life for far too long, and he didn't want to make any mistakes. This adventure could cost him more dearly than any assignment he had ever taken on, and there was no margin for error.

Henry VIII caught Ray's attention just then as he stepped up beside him and set down his plastic turkey leg in order to fill his plate with a real one and some candied yams and chestnut stuffing.

Something he mistook as a finger stroked the back of Ray's thigh and moved upward in a slow, sensual motion. When he whirled around to face it, though, he found himself looking at the back of a shapely kitten whose tail had gone somewhat out of control as she bent over the silver platter of caviar.

Ray quickly loaded his plate and stopped at the bar just outside the door to snatch up one of the dozens of glasses of champagne on golden trays before sitting down on the stone wall that separated the patio from the running stream and waterfall.

"And where is Tonto this fine evening?" a shapely princess inquired.

"Home with a headache," he replied dryly, relieved when she got the message in his disinterest and wandered away.

A soft thump beside him caused Ray to flinch, but only slightly. He gazed casually over at the Captain Hook seated next to him. Upon closer inspection, he realized . . . he knew that pirate.

"Cort," he stated softly, concentrating on the pasta salad on his plate. "I wondered if you would show."

"When the Lone Ranger calls for backup," Cort said hoarsely, "the cavalry better show. Where's the woman?"

"Hotel. What's the lay of the land?"

"Monitors of every nook and cranny on the ground floor, inside and out. The grounds are extensively covered, the party, the parking lot. You've got quite a job ahead of you. But we've got to get our hands on those files to make a case against Carmichael."

"We?" Ray said on a chuckle.

"Okay, you."

"Are you ready to back me up?"

"We're ready. I've got six men on this. Two out the back, two in front, and two around the perimeter. You've got exactly ten minutes inside. If you don't find what you need in those ten minutes, get out anyway. You got me, Ray?"

Ray shot him a smile and nodded, popping a shrimp into his mouth before muttering, "Hi-ho, Silver. Away."

The old familiar rush of exhilaration passed through him like the cool breath of a demon. This was the part of being a cop that he missed. The timing of it. The going in and getting it done. But then his Aunt Grace passed over his memory for a clouded moment, and he remembered how he looked forward to the day when he could return to Walt

Whitman, for good this time. He sent a silent prayer upward that, when he returned, Raine would be at his side. All sins forgiven.

Ray spotted the camera lens indistinctly glaring hard at him from the opposite wall. A deep breath and he was ready. He waited . . . waited . . . and as it made the turn, so did he.

The panel opened exactly as Raine had said that it would, and Ray slipped discreetly inside. For a moment, he felt panic surge up to the surface inside him. He set his watch for precisely ten minutes.

Just get inside and get those files.

He knew they were there, and they were going to put Carmichael away for a very long time. He clung to that as he stepped up to the key pad. It was identical to the sketch Raine had provided. He quickly punched out her birthday. 1-0-1-7, then entered it with the *key. Its response was as it was foretold. A quick buzz and the door slipped open.

Even from the hotel suite miles away, she spurred him on like an angelic spirit guide. He took the turns just as she had instructed him, two rights, and then a sharp left. It was an intricate maze of rooms and corridors, but her instructions hadn't failed him. He reached the next key pad and punched at it confidently.

7-1-0-1. Her birthday, backwards. With a buzz, the door slid open to grant him entrance.

Ray glanced at his watch as he stepped inside. Nearly nine minutes left to go and he was already in. It was better than they'd hoped for. The exact location of the files was one of the few chunks of information Raine hadn't been able to provide, but Ray was determined. He opened drawers beneath the intricate electrical board at random.

There was little more inside many of them besides boxes of slides. Ray removed one and held it up to what little light the room provided and saw that the transparency was of a framed Picasso. Just which one, he couldn't recall.

These could be the forgery records, he deduced. It was good, but not good enough. He didn't want to settle for the hors d'oeuvre when it was the meat he was looking for.

Ray removed the cowboy hat, then the black mask, and set them on the counter beside him. The weight of the gun inside the bowl had begun to make itself known, even though the Derringer was the still the most convenient and lightweight piece available.

At the bottom of the row of drawers, Ray came across one locked drawer. He quickly pulled the small leather case from his boot and began to poke at the bolt that held it shut tight with the tool made just for such instances. He used to be pretty fast at this, he recalled. It shouldn't take more than another moment . . . *Click!*

He sighed as he pulled open the long drawer to reveal the dozens of manila file folders placed neatly inside. This was it!

"That was very good. And in record time too."

Ray felt his heart enlarge inside his chest, and he reeled around to come face to face with a man he had come to despise without ever having laid eyes on him before.

"Carmichael," he spat.

"How nice to be recognized," the swine returned.

There was something foul about the man. Oh, he was smooth, all right. Plenty smooth. But there was a sniveling quality about him, even though he was obviously the one in control. A slight whine to his voice set Ray's teeth on edge.

"Let's take a walk, shall we?" Carmichael suggested as he nodded toward the cowboy suddenly poised just beside him.

He pointed the barrel of a pistol bearing a four-inch silencer right into Ray's face. "Grab your hat, Lone Ranger. It's high noon."

"What a wit," Ray returned sarcastically as he took up

the hat and placed it carefully back on his head, wrapping the mask around his gloved hand.

"Put that on too," he was instructed. "We're going to walk right through the party traffic. Anything funny and a lot of innocent people are going to get hurt," he promised, and Ray believed him.

Ray's mind raced with a hundred different scenarios as they approached the final panel that would lead them out, and he silently thanked the Lord above that he'd landed on that final choice to leave Raine behind. No matter what happened now, at least she was safe.

Glancing at his watch, he noted that there were still four minutes left to go, but Cort was sure to spot him coming out of the room if he was watching as attentively as he hoped. If anyone were going to get him out of this mess, it would have to be Cort, so Ray decided to follow directions at this point and see where it took him. He couldn't get any more caught than he already was, after all.

On their way up the marble staircase to the second floor, Ray noticed the cowboy's gun shrouded by his open suede jacket.

"Inside," the guy barked, and Ray followed his order and crossed through the door at the far right of the hall.

His resolve took a nose-dive as he entered to find Cort seated against the wall, and one of the largest men Ray had ever seen in the flesh standing next to him, gun in massive hand.

"Let's have a look at you."

With the wave of his hand, Carmichael motioned Ray to remove the mask again, which he did, then followed up by removing the hat and placing it carefully down on the seat of the corner chair.

"So this is the fellow who's been traveling with my wife."

And, with that, he raised an unexpected left hook delivered with the added strength of the butt of a pistol right to the center of Ray's face. Pain seemed to scream out inside his head like a blood-curdling reaction in a haunted house. He was sure his nose was broken, and the endless river of blood that followed pretty much confirmed it.

"Where is she?" Carmichael asked, but Ray looked away in silence, considering his next move.

"Well?" he bellowed, and Ray was stunned to realize Carmichael was addressing Cort.

"Martin developed a backbone of chivalry I hadn't anticipated and left her behind," he stated, and a steel rod of realization went straight through Ray.

Cort isn't here because he was caught. He's here because he's . . . a traitor.

"But I've sent Lowe and Douglass over to the hotel to pick her up. It's no big deal."

"Well, it wouldn't have been," a large yellow-haired man squawked from the doorway. "Except she's not there."

"What do you mean, Douglass?" Cort asked nervously, looking back to Carmichael for reaction.

"She was nowhere to be found in that hotel room," the man explained.

Ray struggled to stop the flow of blood from his nose, using the sleeve of his shirt to catch some of it. He wasn't sure if it was the rapid loss of blood or his overwhelming concern for Raine that caused him to swagger slightly on his feet. He felt as if he might black out at any moment, and he fought it good and hard.

"If she's not there, then we know where she's headed," Carmichael replied coldly. And, shooting a glare Ray's way, he added, "Don't we, Officer Martin?"

Chapter Fourteen

Ray's stare could have broken Cort into a thousand fragmented pieces from where he was seated. He couldn't believe his instincts had gone so bad.

"Mr. Carmichael," the monstrosity with the gun said in a raspy voice. "Take a look."

All eyes turned toward the monitor on the lower left corner of the board. In black and white, it was hard to spot the figure moving rapidly through the darkness across the lawn toward the house. It had appeared out of the woods and moved spryly over the grass. The figure was cloaked in black and might have gone unnoticed under other circumstances.

"Well, well." Carmichael grinned from ear to ear. "She's still in quite good shape, isn't she?"

Ray froze as he watched the screen. He would know that form anywhere. Dressed like a cat burglar, including the ski mask, she had probably thought she could pass for one of the costumed guests if spotted.

Oh, Raine. What were you thinking, coming back here?

"She'll come back into the house the same way she left," Carmichael told them, never removing his eyes from

171

Raine's form on the screen. "Lowe and Douglass, you plant yourselves outside. One of you by the trellis, the other near the woods. Laird will stay here and watch over them. No one leaves this room."

"Leave her alone," Ray said in a menacing growl.

"This is a reunion long overdue," he growled back. "My beloved wife and I have some catching up to do."

Ray had no control over the force with which he rose to his feet and leapt toward Carmichael. Laird was first to reach him and pulled him back with such force that he slammed against the wall and fell to the floor.

Instinctively, Ray thought to reach for the gun taped into the band of his hat, but he knew there was no way he would be able to produce it in time to stop Carmichael. All he would succeed in doing would be to tip his own hand. And since he was holding only one ace at the moment, he held himself back.

Carmichael arrogantly brushed the arm of his jacket as if he were flicking away a particle of dust.

"Don't ever touch me again, Martin," he warned. "Or you'll be dead on the spot."

"Damn!"

The trellis was no longer in place, and Raine quickly darted around the corner of the house. Shielding herself in the cover of the landscape, she conformed to the wall, catching her breath as she considered her next move.

She'd given Ray all of the information that she'd had, from the floor plan to the codes, but she didn't feel confident that it was enough to make up for his never having been inside the house before. She, on the other hand, knew the place by heart, even after so many precious months free from its walls. If she could just find him, she could make sure he got in and out of the place, as quickly as possible.

It was then that Raine realized . . . She was no longer

angry at Ray for having left her behind in the hotel room, nor for having destroyed the costume that was to gain her entry. She had even forgiven him for breaking his word.

All she cared about . . . the only concern looming large inside her trembling and terrified heart . . . was that she and Ray lived through this night. Every hope for the future danced on that one lone fact. She hadn't known it then, but she knew it now . . . every road she'd taken, every step she'd made in all of her life, had been a part of the journey that had led her straight to Ray Martin's arms. In those arms, she was whole. She was fulfilled. She was home, and she'd found love. The love that she now felt certain God had intended for her, all along.

Nothing was going to rob her of that love now! Nothing. She couldn't even entertain the notion that she could lose it before it had really begun, while it was so new, while there was still so much to be discovered! Fresh resolve surged through her, and Raine swallowed hard over the lump of fear at the center of her throat.

She peeked around the corner cautiously, praying that the second trellis at the other side of the mansion hadn't been removed as well. Crouching along the shell of the house, she noiselessly made her way toward the front. And just as she poised herself to take that final step toward the trellis to the roof, something latched on to her shoulder and swooped her smoothly to the ground.

"Welcome home, Mrs. Carmichael," he whispered, and then the one she remembered as the Baboon yanked the ski mask from her head and pounced on top of her, shoving the air out of her lungs with mighty force.

His monkey face stared down at her, and his big apelike hands with the hairy knuckles she remembered so well held her securely to the ground. Suddenly, there had been no time that had passed since the night he had followed behind them, Raine kicking and screaming and biting to no avail as Harrison dragged her by the hair down the hallway to that wretched bedroom she'd once known so well, despised so much.

He carried her under one arm like a sack of potatoes, his free hand tangled into her hair, clutching it so that she couldn't move her head at all. She could hardly breathe, and it was impossible for her to reposition in a way that she could catch sight of who it was that helped him as he stuffed her into what felt like a harsh burlap bag.

She struggled against the fabric, trying with all her might to get free, and a sudden thump to the side of her head nearly knocked her unconscious. Raine fought against the reeling senses, shutting her eyes and shaking it free.

"Hey!" she shouted. "That hurt, you . . . you . . . *Baboon*!"

In just another moment's time, she fell to the ground with a thud and, when the fabric parted just above her head, she sucked desperately at the blessed air until she choked on it.

The Baboon scooped her up from the floor and lifted her to her feet, then released her so abruptly that she nearly fell right back down again.

"You're not looking your best this evening, Lorraine."

Raine spun around toward the voice that had been haunting her over the months since she'd escaped, and she shoved the tangled mat of hair from her eyes as she did.

"But welcome home."

It seemed to Ray that Carmichael had been gone for hours. He'd heard a clamor down the hall at one point and he strained to listen but never heard another sound above the music wafting up the stairs from the party below.

He'd been able to work the tape free from the gun inside the silly Lone Ranger hat beside him without being discovered and had placed it loose on the floor, the hat concealing it until full advantage presented itself.

He was so worried about Raine that his stomach was tied in knots. And his disappointment in Cort's alliance with Carmichael sliced through him with a cold steel blade. How could he have missed that possibility?

When the door opened and Carmichael shoved Raine through ahead of him, Ray felt the planet rock beneath him.

One piece of luck in an otherwise complete bomb of a day. She's alive. For the moment, Raine is still alive.

When she lifted her eyes for the first time and focused on him, slumped to the floor next to the wall, Ray had meant to shoot her a look of hope. Instead, it came out as a slight cringe.

Blood was everywhere around him, and his nose was misshapen and probably bruised by now. He knew how horrifying he must have looked to her simply by the sheer terror that rose in her eyes at the sight of him.

"Oh my God," she whispered, raising her hand to her own face in sympathy-pain. "Are you all right?"

"I'll live." He tried to smile reassuredly, but she didn't look like she believed him.

"Let's not be so hasty." Harrison laughed. "You may or may not live. That's really up to me, isn't it?"

Carmichael led Raine up by an elbow and deposited her delicately in the chair Cort vacated.

"Where is everyone?" Carmichael asked him.

"Lowe and Douglass are downstairs. Kane is securing the files."

"Here's what I thought would be fun," Harrison told Cort with a demented lilt to his voice. "I'm going to dispose of my wife's new love. What do you think of that, Officer Martin?"

Ray didn't reply, but he felt the weight of Raine's gasp all the way to his toes.

"No," she cried, and the goon that looked alarmingly like a large ape tucked her back down into the chair.

"Dear boy, runaway wives can always assure you of one thing. If they have something to run to, they will continue to run away. Lorraine is not going to run away again. Are you, darling?"

Raine didn't answer, but her eyes met Ray's for a long moment.

Raine tried to read the message in Ray's eyes, to find an answer somewhere beyond the blood and confusion. He was her only source of strength, and she was grateful that he didn't pull his gaze away from her before she was able to continue drawing from it. Like water from a well, his dark brown eyes refreshed her. There was a promise there. She couldn't put a name to it, but it was a promise just the same. Something was going to happen at any moment, she could feel it.

Suddenly, things began to move so quickly that Raine couldn't keep up. Ray lunged toward Laird and the slippery clank of a silencer-induced gunshot sounded, then full shots rang out from more than one direction.

"I'm one of the good guys," one of the men shouted, and Ray heaved out a relieved smile before shouting, "Raine, get down!"

She dropped immediately to the floor and crawled beneath the desk in time to see Ray produce a tiny handgun and pelt several bullets out of it.

It was surrealistic. Unreal. Everything was moving in slow motion, like the *Bonnie and Clyde* movie she'd seen once with her girlfriends at a retrospective on gangsters at the local drive-in theater. Gunshots exploded from around the room and then, a moment later, the room fell silent and someone dropped to the floor in front of Raine, his eyes bulging and a shocked expression peering up at her from where he'd landed.

When the shooting stopped, Ray crawled toward her.

"Raine," he whispered, and she moved into his arms. "Will you be all right here?"

"No," she pleaded. "Don't leave me."

"Harrison has escaped. We can't let him slip through our fingers now."

"Can you use this thing?" someone asked her, then one of the men she'd thought worked for Harrison placed Cort's gun into her hand.

"Yes," Ray answered for her. "She can."

"Sit tight," the man instructed her. "And shoot anything that moves."

"Unless it's one of us," Ray added. "Don't leave this room. I'll be back for you."

"Zacharias Kane," the stranger stated as he slapped Ray hard on the arm. "I've been undercover here for three months. I had a feeling about Cort."

"What about the men posted outside?"

"They're Bureau, through and through, as far as I know. If we move fast, we might have a shot at capturing Carmichael."

She wanted to beg him not to leave her. To just let Harrison run, to pick her up into those strong arms of his and hurry from this place for the last time. As fast as they could run. Into the woods and over the fence. She'd done it once, and she could do it again. But something stopped her. She silently watched him leave the room behind Kane, and she clutched the gun to her chest, shutting her eyes as tightly as she could.

"Please God," she prayed out loud. "Help us get out of here alive. Make this thing end once and for all."

"Yes, God, please do."

She snapped open her eyes to find Harrison standing over

her and she instinctively raised the gun toward him as the sound of sirens moved in toward the house.

"Go ahead," he seemed to invite her. "Let's go out together, Lorraine."

"Just stay back," she warned him, then called out, "Ray!"

"Don't," he pleaded with her as he lowered himself slowly to the floor to face her. "I can forgive you, Lorraine. Only don't call out to him. Don't bring him between us again."

"Ray!" she called louder.

"No!" he said sharply. "Come here to me, Lorraine."

As he raised his hand toward her, Raine recoiled. "Stay back, Harrison."

"Come here to me, darling."

Their eyes locked for a long moment, and she recognized the flames of anger beginning to rise inside him. She'd seen it far too many times.

"Harrison, just back off. Back away from me."

"Give me the gun, Lorraine!" he ordered and, when she didn't heed his command, he lurched forward toward her.

Raine squeezed the trigger without blinking, and she watched Harrison collapse in a heavy mound right into her lap.

Long moments hissed by, and Raine was frozen solid. She couldn't even feel herself breathing. And then the thump of activity down the hall jostled her. Her eyes fluttered, her heart began to beat again, and someone shoved Harrison over on his back to the floor.

"Lorraine," he wheezed out at her, and she closed her eyes and turned away from him.

"Raine!"

"Ray?" she managed in a raspy voice that she didn't recognize herself.

"Shhhhh," he comforted her as he took her into his arms,

anointing her with an array of tiny kisses across her fore-head and over the top of her skull.

Raine forced shut her eyes, and they stung as she did.

"Are you all right?" she asked him.

"I'm fine," he chuckled. "Just fine."

"Thank God."

"He'll never hurt you again," he vowed to her. "And that's a promise I swear I won't break."

Chapter Fifteen

"Maybe we should have called ahead," Raine repeated for the 10th time at least. "The way you look, Ray. It could scare her."

Ray took a quick glance at his bandaged nose in the rear view, and then he shot a slanted smile her way. He did look quite a sight, after all! His nose was bandaged, and so were his ribs, and when he'd walked off the plane just that morning, he'd done so with quite a significant limp.

As the car rounded the curve toward the house, he noticed Grace sitting in her usual spot in the old wicker chair at the corner of the porch. As they approached, Grace rose and hurriedly struggled down the steps to the yard.

"Raymond!" she called out, waving frantically. "Raine, dear!"

"Grace!"

"Puppet, my puppet." Grace sighed as they embraced, and Ray joined them in the huddle. "Thank you, Jesus," she cried again and again. "Thank you for bringing my children home to me."

After a long moment, she pulled from them and looked Ray right in the eye with a grin. "What took you so long?"

"We had a few things to take care of, Gracie," he chuckled.

"I've been waiting here all day!"

"You knew we were coming then?" Raine asked curiously. "How?"

"Hello!"

They all three turned to find Zacharias Kane nodding to them from the front porch as he ran a hand through his blondstreaked hair. "What took you so long?" he called out, and his very blue eyes glistened in the sun.

"What are you doing here?" Raine asked happily.

"Do you have news from the department?" Ray inquired.

"You know that Carmichael is dead?"

"Yes," Ray replied softly. "They told us."

"Cort was brought in the night of the masquerade ball," Kane said as he approached, "and he's singing like a bird. About everything. And Carmichael's files are in department hands. It looks like a happy ending after all."

"Oh, thank God," Raine said, and Ray wrapped her up with one arm and pulled her close to him.

"I'm also here to extend an invitation to you, Ray. What would you say about coming to work for the Bureau?"

Raine looked up at him so quickly that he nearly felt her neck snap.

"We're going to take care of that sticky issue out of your past, and you'll be cleared of all charges within the week."

"Oh, Ray!" Raine sang excitedly. "That's wonderful."

Relief washed over him in sprays and waves. He'd waited a very long time to hear those words.

"You'll be needing a job, won't you?"

Raine looked up at him again, and he could feel her tremble slightly.

"I have a job, Zach," he replied.

"Look, I've seen surveillance photos of that office of yours. You—"

"I'm going to be opening a bed and breakfast with my wife," he interrupted.

Raine's squeals of joy were music to his ears, and Ray managed to catch her just as she leaped into both of his arms, and then he cried out in a groan of pain.

"Ooooh, your ribs! I'm sorry. Oh, Ray."

"It's okay. It's okay."

Zach grinned at them, and placed an arm around Grace's shoulder.

"Maybe I'll stick around for the wedding," he said softly. "When is it?"

"The sooner the better," Ray chimed in.

"As soon as he can walk down the aisle without limping." Raine laughed and looked hard into Ray's now-serious eyes.

"I'd marry you if I had to crawl down the aisle," he told her, and he could see that she believed him all the way to the bottom of her soul.

"Any more adventures and you may have to do just that!" Zach teased.

"Bite your tongue, dear," Grace added.

"I love you so much," Raine whispered to Ray, and he took her into his arms and held her to him so close that he could feel her heart pounding against him. She didn't seem to notice as Ray winced one more time.

It was a strain for him to cling to her, but he did it anyway. After all they'd been through to get there, it was an impossibility not to.